Mississippi Blues

Mississippi Blues

CASSANDRA DARDEN BELL

sepia
BET
BOOKS

BET Publications, LLC
http://www.bet.com

SEPIA BOOKS are published by

BET Publications, LLC
c/o BET BOOKS
One BET Plaza
1900 W Place NE
Washington, DC 20018-1211

All Kensington Titles, Imprints, and Distributed Lines are available at special quantity discounts for bulk purchases for sales promotions, premiums, fund-raising, and educational or institutional use. Special book excerpts or customized printings can also be created to fit specific needs. For details, write or phone the office of the Kensington special sales manager: Kensington Publishing Corp., 850 Third Avenue, New York, NY 10022, attn: Special Sales Department, Phone: 1-800-221-2647.

ISBN: 1-58314-481-1

First Printing: January 2004
10 9 8 7 6 5 4 3 2 1

Printed in the United States of America

In Memory of
Ronald D. Smith
March 12, 1949–June 17, 2000
Joy R. Smith "See It a Different Way" eulogy

Acknowledgments

Special thanks to my agent Sha Shana Crichton for her dedication, expertise, and friendship. To my editor, Glenda Howard, thanks for your wisdom and guidance in helping me to get my point across. My mother Lillie, and mother-in-law Frances . . . thanks for too many things to mention, to two moms who know their children will always need them. Thanks to Laura Hamilton (Hair Unique), Lola Thompson (True Connections Spa), and Ann Speight . . . these ladies make my bland vanilla into luscious, creamy French Vanilla. My sincere appreciation to my mentor, Dr. Seodial Deena, East Carolina University, Eve Rodgers and AIM, Kevin Kane and Latisha Speaks, the Gershwins, Lauryn, Ariel, Jordan, and last but not least, my knight in shining armor . . . Larry Bell. Thank you, sweetheart, for toiling with me through the process. When the day is done, everyone else gets to go home, but we are forever in this together!

Chapter 1

"Noooo," I growled, with the alarm clock blaring in my ear. After knocking over books, reading glasses, and papers, I fumbled my way to the alarm's OFF button. I pulled the pillow back over my head, dreading the inevitable. At 6:30 in the morning, any respectable person would have given herself at least another half hour to sleep. But Junior had to be at basketball camp by 7:30, and Lisa was taking the SAT at 8:00 sharp.

I slid my hand to the other side of the king-sized Valencia sleigh bed to confirm what I already knew. He was gone. Of course he was. He never stayed in bed past 5:00 AM, even during the cold winter months when snow would likely shut down all activity for the day. I ran my hand up and down the cool cotton sheets until I felt the rough fabric of the quilted, honey wheat–toned comforter on his side of the bed. Without even turning to look, my hand confirmed what my heart already knew. What was I thinking? Did I actually think I'd find his warm body still lying there waiting for a little early morning nooky?

"Hell no," I mumbled as I pulled the pillow off my head and looked anyway. No Michael. No nooky. Only two kids with appointments that they didn't dare miss and one mother who desperately needed to get her ass in gear.

As I stumbled from the bed toward the bathroom, I stopped briefly to see if I heard any sound of life downstairs. Of course not. I certainly didn't expect to hear two teenagers fixing breakfast with pleasant smiles and kind words. They were both probably still in bed, wanting nothing to do with 6:30 in the morning. I decided it was too soon to face their bad breath and attitudes to match. I'd take a shower first.

At thirty-seven years old, I was still holding my own, I thought as I glanced in the mirror. I wasn't too disappointed by the woman looking back—a good-looking woman, considering hair going every which way and dried-up white stuff in the corners of her eyes. The bags under her eyes weren't nearly as bad as most of the women her age, and breasts . . . still perky enough to get a second look.

"Whewwww," I sighed, realizing the bad-breath monster was all up in my grill this morning. I reached into the shower, grabbed the cold-water knob, and gave it a quick turn, then did the same thing to the hot water. The routine was the same every day. I stepped into the shower built for two and let the water run over my naked, yearning body.

"Shower built for two," I laughed, thinking of the irony of it. It was a nice shower, I thought as I looked around the 6'4" box I had seen every day for the last ten years of my life. The tile was a kelly green faux marble finish. I looked at the custom-built lighting and ventilation unit. It was trimmed in stainless steel. "Top-of-the-line stuff that won't ever rust or fade," I remembered the salesman telling us. I let the water run down my neck, over my hardened nipples, as I realized how many years I had been enjoying this shower built for two, all alone.

In one swift motion, I toweled off and grabbed the first thing I came to in the closet—a pair of blue jeans. Button-fly Levi's and a pale blue T-shirt were just fine for the day ahead of me. I glanced at the Donna Karan dresses and Louis Vuitton shoes and handbags as I pulled the jeans and T-shirt off the rack. I pulled the jeans on, looking back at all the fancy clothes. They reminded me of the boring dinner parties and fund-raisers we had attended since Michael made partner. Too many snobby, highly educated legal eagles in one place would automatically spell boredom for most folk, but for me, it was my saving grace. But this morning I couldn't think about the dinners, the expensive shoes, or phony know-it-alls at Michael's firm. No, today it was more than I could bring myself to care about.

By the time I got the jeans on and the shirt over my head, my bedroom door eased open and I waited for my favorite morning visitor.

"Come on in, Bessie. Come here, baby, Mommy wants some lovin' from her baby."

Bessie is my overweight, one-foot-in-the-grave Siamese cat, named for the famous jazz singer Bessie Smith. She's likely used up at least seven of her nine lives, and I can't imagine living life without her. Old faithful. Once again, she'd made it up the stairs and into my room to greet me with warm fur and a faint purr. She slithered around my ankles while I continued making a big deal out of her as if we didn't go through this every day.

"Come on, sweet pea, give Mommy a kiss," I begged as she finally jumped into my lap, barely clearing my left leg.

I grabbed her huge backside and gave her a little shove. She snuggled into my lap, rubbing her head against the wrinkled cotton fabric of the blue jeans. Watching her motions, I almost felt like facing the day.

"It would be nice if you showed *us* that much attention in the morning, Ma."

Lisa had risen from the dead and was standing in my doorway, watching my Bessie moment.

"If you were half as sweet as this one is, I might just do that," I teased.

3

Lisa is my sixteen-year-old. I call her my "just after the honeymoon baby." Michael and I had hardly been married six months when I found out I was pregnant with Lisa. As a baby, she was the cutest thing I had ever seen. She'd look at me with those innocent baby eyes and melt my heart. At sixteen she was still a cutie, but my deepest fears told me the innocence was long gone. She flopped down on my bed wearing a nightshirt that fell just short enough to reveal a pair of thong underwear.

"Girl, where the hell did you get them drawers?" I yelled before realizing they were mine.

She covered herself, too embarrassed and too proud to start discussing why she felt the need to put my sexy underwear on her fast teenage behind. I'd deal with her later. The clock was ticking and I still hadn't gotten my first dose of caffeine. Lisa made a quick exit, wanting desperately to avoid the underwear conversation.

"Ma, you know I have to be there at eight, I mean in the building at eight, not driving up," Lisa yelled as she went back down the hall to her own room to get dressed.

"Yes, Miss Thang, I know what time you have to be there. You just get yourself ready . . . and take my drawers off," I yelled, following her into the hallway.

Junior was coming out of his room just in time to hear me yelling about my underwear. He shook his head and went on about his business as if I were just another stranger on the street.

"And good morning to you, young man, I don't recall us sleeping in the same bed."

"Mornin', Ma," he said with a half smile that let me know that was as much as I would get from him at 7:00 in the morning.

I watched Junior go into the bathroom and shut the door before making my way further into the dismal swamp of my morning routine. The back stairs that led to the kitchen were right beside my bedroom, so that was the route I took each morning. Five steps, then a slight forty-five-degree turn and seven more steps led to the kitchen. The sun was already beaming into the tiny kitchen decorated in country gingham pattern. I'd hated those damn hens and ducks from day one, but Michael's mother always had a country kitchen, so anything else would have been out of the question.

"A kitchen is supposed to give you a certain feeling, Bev," he would always say.

This kitchen was certainly doing just that. The feeling wasn't good. Too much light blue and yellow. And who the hell wants to look at a gingham pattern while trying to eat? Getting angry wasn't going to make the ducks fade, so I started my coffee routine.

The routine was always the same. I could do it without a second thought. Pull the Mr. Coffee deluxe machine out to the center of the countertop, flip the door for the grains and empty the old filter from the machine. I always planned to take the old filter out after finishing a pot, but the good intentions never amounted to much. Besides, who'd care if I left the old grains in the filter or not? Open the cabinet just above my head, pull out freshly ground coffee . . . four scoops, five scoops, and a little more for good measure. Fill the pot with water, pour it into the chamber, put the pot back on the burner, and hit the ON button.

The soft gurgling sound started immediately. Most days I opened the curtain at the kitchen sink window, just to get a glimpse of the day. But not this particular day. There was no use. It was another day, I had stuff to do, weather wasn't going to change that so why look out the window? I walked to the cabinet to get my favorite coffee mug. Avid coffee drinkers always have a mug. In fact, everyone in our house has his or her special mug. My mug says I IS A REAL WRITER. The kids gave it to me as a joke a few years back and I've used it ever since. But today, I let the mug sit in its spot. I didn't feel like the best-selling author of ten mystery novels, but more like a washed out, lonely old woman. The "writer mug" didn't seem appropriate. I needed something more. I went to my china cabinet and grabbed one of my Wedgwood cups.

"Fine china is okay on a Tuesday in July," I mumbled as if I needed to justify using my own china.

Knowing full well the cup wasn't going to change one thing, I poured the coffee; strong, black, steaming liquid hit my tongue with a sensation that would make the average person pant. I continued sipping and staring at nothing in particular, sipping and staring until the cup was empty and the hot liquid bubbled in my empty stomach.

"Same shit, different day," I whispered, as I poured another cup.

Chapter 2

"Come on, girl, I have to drop your brother off and get back across town so you won't be late," I yelled to Lisa while turning the key in the ignition of my golden pearl Lexus LX 470.

I revved the truck engine to give Lisa a signal to get her butt into gear. She jumped into the back seat, rolling her eyes at her brother. They'd been doing this mess since Junior was a toddler—fighting over the front seat in the car. The game would start as soon as I announced we were going someplace. One of them would yell, "I've got front seat," trying to get the words out faster than the other. The challenge was over when one victoriously shouted the phrase first, until Junior got big enough to challenge Lisa physically. Then the game went to a whole new level. It became a test of who could actually get to the vehicle faster and shove the other out of the way and forcibly take over the seat. I tried too many times to stop the action, but after ten years, the front-seat game was their thing and I stayed out of it.

"You only got it 'cause I had to go back and get my bag."

"No, I got it 'cause you can't move in those tight panties," Junior taunted.

I smiled and pulled out of the driveway, trying not to think about

Lisa wearing those underwear out of the house. As we drove down the street and approached the stop sign at the end of Lincoln Street, I realized I was listening to gospel music.

"Who the hell set the station to gospel music?" I questioned.

"Ma, they play some def jams at night. They play that church stuff in the morning when no one really listens anyway," Lisa explained.

As I reached down to turn the station to something worth listening to, a man with a Southern drawl much like the folk in my hometown in Mississippi started to belt out a creaky version of "Lord Don't Move My Mountain." I knew the song before he could go on. I had heard that one too many times at the old Baptist church back home. "Lord don't move my mountain, just give me the strength to climb." I hit the SEARCH button before he could get the word "climb" out of his mouth.

"Who the hell wants to climb a damn mountain," I said to myself just as I came across the oldies station—my kind of music. Bobby Womack was hitting the bridge of "If You Think You're Lonely Now," and I couldn't help but shout a big amen. I may not know much about the Lord and climbing mountains, but I know about being lonely.

"Sing it Bobby, baby," I teased, knowing that would get a reaction from both Junior and Lisa.

They didn't put up a fight about the station since neither of them would be in the car for long, forced to listen to Mama's "old-folks music," as they called it. After dropping Junior off at the school, I drove to the other side of Melrose to drop Lisa off at the office building where they were administering the test. She jumped out and I watched her little behind shaking as she made her way up the walkway and into the front door. She was definitely wearing my drawers or none at all. Not a panty line in sight. *Fast tail.* I drove off, heading—where else—back home.

As I drove past the strip mall near the house, I noticed the nail shop owner opening her front door. Nails by Nelly was supposed to be one of the best nail shops in town, but I had yet to stop by and pay Nelly a visit. I thought of stopping in to get a manicure—something different, a nice pale pink shade to match my casual weekday wardrobe, or perhaps a bright red, kind of daring with a little hint of adventure.

"Naaa," I mouthed as I passed and threw a hand up at Nelly. "Not my style."

Nelly, on the other hand, was something else. I had met her months ago at one of the fund-raising dinners that Michael's firm required us to attend. Her husband Howard was with the firm too and he was just as boring as the other 200 or so attorneys that made up Kensey, Nelson and Branch. Nelly's nail business is just her way of keeping out of trouble, or her front for what Nelly really likes to do with her time. Rumor has it, ole Nelly is doing her yardman Hal. It's common knowledge among the wives and I think she's proud of her little fling, especially since Hal is as gorgeous as the day is long. I smiled as I pulled into my driveway. *I may have to get myself a gardener.*

By then, Marvin Gaye was putting it down on some "Sexual Healing," so I couldn't get out of the truck yet. *Got to get all the sexual healing I can, and Marvin's singing will have to do for now.* I turned the truck off and left the key in the ignition, bopping my head to Marvin.

For whatever reason, after a few seconds even Marvin's sultry sound couldn't keep my mind off how bad things were. Not bad according to most people's definition. We have all the money we need. The bills are paid, my sixteen-year-old daughter and fourteen-year-old son are in good health and doing well in school. The kids are not in any trouble that we know of; we have a lovely home, three new vehicles and a boat. So why the hell am I so miserable? Michael is a successful attorney; I am a best-selling author. So why can't I get out of the truck and go into that lovely home and get to work?

By the time I snapped out of my daze, Marvin was long done

with his healing and a commercial for Preparation H was talking about getting rid of that painful burn and itch. That was reason enough to get out of the car. As I walked up the drive toward the back door, I took in all that made up my home in Melrose, Massachusetts. I remembered when we bought the house. Michael had been immediately sold by all the space. The home was older, with its own unique character, but all he'd commented on was the amount of space for the price. He was convinced we were getting a deal. There were eleven rooms total on two stories and a basement. The master bedroom and four other bedrooms were all on the second floor. What the hell did we need with five bedrooms? The living room, dining room, family room, and kitchen were all on the ground floor, and then there was that awful basement. I'd hated it on sight. It was dark and musty with an ugly green slime all over the walls. Michael mentioned turning it into a writing area for me. I laughed at the thought of writing in that cave. Most writers want to be close to nature, not buried alive.

That was nearly fifteen years before, and not only had I been buried alive, I had learned not to bang on the walls to get out. The wood, cement, and studs were now covered by paint, wallpaper, and carpet to form a haven, a work space, a place for creative narrative to explode, but it wasn't real. Nothing about it was real. And I was afraid someone would find out about my troublesome spot of solitude and loneliness.

The big clock over the couch in the den said it was 8:30. As a full-time writer I try to make sure I'm seated at my desk in the cave at least by 9:00 each morning. This morning, going into that cave was the last thing on my mind. It was too early to have a drink, but my mouth was in need of something hard to ease the pain in my chest, the longing in my heart. I walked past the couch and looked at the clock again: 8:31. I flopped down on the double-arm chaise positioned between the fireplace and the bay window. As I reached over to pull the curtain back, the notion struck me to ask Michael about taking a vacation—not anything big, just a long weekend away. We could leave on Thursday, go someplace romantic—no kids, just the two of us. I could hear the excuses in my head. I had heard them time and time again.

"Bev, you know I'm in the middle of the Wilhelm case," or maybe it was an important meeting with the partners.

"I know three days don't seem like much, but I can't even spare three hours right now," he would say on his way out the door.

I talked myself out of mentioning it. We had done it before, but that was seven years ago now. *It was our anniversary and I had gotten him to take three days away. We drove up to Maine and checked into a little bed-and-breakfast. As I unpacked little nighties and skimpy dresses, Michael set up his laptop on the table beside the bed. I fought back the tears, but didn't complain about the computer. After he logged on and checked his e-mails, he shut it down so we could have dinner. I used my best creative plotting and devised a plan to get him away from that computer at least for one night. I had the innkeeper call the room and tell him the phone lines would be down for the rest of the night but should be back up in the morning. Supposedly, they were having some minor repair work done.*

It worked. Michael and I had dinner, returned to the room, and instead of the laptop, I was the one getting the "hard drive." We made love like we did when we first met. We talked and laughed about crazy things the kids did around the house. At the stroke of midnight, our official ten-year wedding anniversary, he gave me a gold compact with the sweetest inscription. We sipped wine, slept in each other's arms, and made love every time we woke up. As I drifted off to sleep at 4:30 in the morning, I could feel myself falling in love again. I was sure we were getting a fresh start, until I woke up the next morning and found him nervously checking the phone lines and logging on. As wonderful as the night had been, I faced the stark reality that nothing had changed and the few hours of passion we shared had been just that—a few hours.

The chiming grandfather clock startled me as it sounded its familiar tune. I looked at the clock, realizing it was time to go to work. Nine o'clock on the dot. I grabbed a bottled water from the fridge and made my way to the cave.

The cave had changed over the years. Right before Junior was born, I got into one of those nesting fits and cleaned all the green slime off the walls. I cleaned the floors and had plush wall-to-wall velvet blue carpet laid down. Michael was against it since the basement had a damp feel. He thought carpet would start to smell over time.

"Well, I'll just get new carpet," I argued, willing to do anything to soften up things in what would become my home away from home.

The walls were covered in an elegant wallpaper pattern of light blues and mauve. It brightened up the room wonderfully. I painted the ceiling white to add light from above and had recessed lighting installed throughout the room. I painted the old radiator and dressed it up so it fit right into the surroundings. I kept it simple in the cave. I had a reading area, stocked with my best friends: McMillan, Sparks, Roberts and Grisham. Whenever I felt like throwing in the towel, one of those guys would slap some sense into me. I had a few magazines in my area, but magazines usually ended up in Lisa's room instead of my magazine rack where they were supposed to be. I glanced over and, sure enough, my latest issue of *O*, Oprah's magazine, was missing in action.

My writing area was a little more intense. It was where I did the dirty work. There was the standard cherry oak desk, credenza and file cabinet. I had a barrister bookcase off to the side of my writing area for all my really important writing tools. It's where I keep my dictionary, Strunk and White, and books personally autographed by writers I've met over the years.

The furniture pieces were surrounded by fake plants because live ones would not survive in the cave. There was also a small table between the desk and wall. That table had a few things on it that meant something to only me. I changed the items periodically, but some of the things always stayed. It was my inspiration table. As I looked around the cave then, wondering how to get out from under the heavy burden, I peered at my table for help.

I walked over and wiped the dust from a picture of my father. It was an early picture of him, before he married Mama. He was maybe sixteen in the picture. Back then it was hard for poor black people to get pictures taken, so this was the only one my dad had for himself that young. When he died, it was one of the things I took. It reminded me of a happier time and place. Most days, just looking at it gave me strength, but not even Daddy could pull me out today. I touched the corner of the frame, wiped away the last streak of dust, and put it back down. I flopped down behind my desk in the high-back Italian leather executive chair. My eyes fell on the print of an old-world map hanging on the wall across from my desk. The "Ivanne Circa Blaeu" historical map had been textured to look authentic and was accented with a linen matte and a cherry finished hardwood frame; one of my most prized pieces, it added a more intellectual style to the room. I studied the map, wishing I were anywhere except Melrose, Massachusetts. It was too early for alcohol—unless you were alone, in a cave.

I went back upstairs and mixed a little peach schnapps with Sprite; nothing too hard for so early in the morning. The cave was not doing much for my mood, and writing was the last thing on my mind, so I flung my body back onto the chaise, sat the drink on the bowlegged drumstool accent table, and looked out the window. Bessie finally made her way back downstairs and joined me on the soft cushion. She looked out the window for a minute and then just curled up around my feet. Her warm fur was the perfect little blanket for my bare size tens. Just as we were about to make ourselves comfortable in that position, a pile of mail came sliding through the mail chute and spread out on the floor at the base of the front door. Bessie and I watched the envelopes slide across the floor, but neither of us moved. I didn't expect her to move, but she tilted her head back and looked at me as if to say, "Aren't you gonna get that?"

Sorting through the mail is one of those things I dread, because I have to do it my way. It's only one of my strange habits, but it can be time-consuming. I looked at the clock again, 10:00, so I decided sorting mail might be a good thing to take up some of the time. I started my ritual. I have to open all my mail first and then go back and read through it piece by piece after it is sitting in front of me, lined up like soldiers going off to battle. That's right, I open every piece, junk mail and all, and then I lay it out in front of me. Then I randomly start to read each piece, cleverly sorting them into piles according to urgency and subject. The bills all go together in my pile of "people that want something from me, and I have to give it to them." The next pile is for "people who want something from me, but I have no obligation to them." That pile sits around for a week and then I usually just trash it. The last pile is for junk mail, but it isn't really a pile because I just toss it straight into file thirteen. To answer your question, yes, I know the bills from the junk when I first open them, but I have to follow my ritual or my entire day will be off. Or at least that's what my mind tells me.

This pile of mail was no different from most; plenty of junk, a few bills, and then I saw it. It was a letter from my sister Mabel. I recognized the handwriting. Mabel has very distinguishable handwriting for an adult. It's cursive true enough, but big swooping letters like a grade-schooler just learning to make their letters. "Dear Bev" took up two lines on the loose-leaf paper and there wasn't much written after it, fortunately, because not much more could fit on the page.

>*Dear Bev, dey called me d'other day and say we need to do somepin bout Daddy nem land or the state gonna step in. Can you come home for a few days and go wit me to fine out what dey talkin bout? Call me at Dashena house 555-2401, cause my phone off again.*
>*Luv,*
>*Mabel*

I held the letter for a while, not sure which pile to put it in. I don't get too many personal letters at my house since my staff handles all the fan mail and correspondences from a post office in another city. My mail is usually just what my piles are designed for. This letter didn't fit nicely into the piles, yet I knew I couldn't just toss it. Mabel needed me.

I was already down in the mouth about my lackluster marriage, and now this. With everything else going wrong in my life, I'd have to deal with Mabel, that land back home, and the ignorant-ass brothers and sisters I vowed never to speak to again after Daddy's funeral.

Chapter 3

Who am I and how did I end up in Melrose, Massachusetts? Well, my pen name is Beverly Bradford Dunn. My real name is Beverly Tayloe Lamark. I started writing novels nearly fifteen years ago and found out, like many brand-new African-American writers, it ain't so easy to make it in this business. I started out trying to tell "our story"; you know, the story of the African-American couple living in America going through their day-to-day struggles of raising a family and trying to make a better life for the next generation. Everything I pitched, bombed. I switched my angles and tried the mystery angle, only with an African-American twist. That was a joke. There's no mystery to it. Who killed the crack ho down the street? My guess is the drug dealer she got the stuff from and couldn't pay. Most of my characters' lives weren't mysterious at all—dysfunctional maybe, but not mysterious. I was failing miserably, so I decided to try one more angle.

Since Michael had become a partner with a firm in Boston, we spent most of our evenings entertaining or being entertained by his colleagues and potential clients. His forte was corporate law. Yes, it was as boring as it sounds, but my saving grace had been all the mess that goes on in corporate America. White-collar crime, mixed with a little sexual scandal and a murder, or kidnapping, makes for the perfect "whodunit." So, ten years earlier I became Beverly Bradford Dunn, best-selling author of *Disgruntled Wives Club*.

My first book was a story about a group of disgruntled wives of corporate gurus who formed a little club and amused themselves by committing crimes, just to see how much they could get away with. First a little forgery and embezzling, and then someone gets in the way and has to be killed. Between trying to figure out who was sleeping with whom and how it related to the murder, I had found my niche and the world of mystery writing would never be the same.

By choice, I didn't make public appearances. I didn't do book signings and talk shows, and I've never had to. The readers loved the books and it added a little suspense to the whole idea, since no one has ever actually seen Beverly Bradford Dunn. My publishing company had one editor who dealt with me and no one else at the company even knew who I was. My editor and I only communicated via phone and e-mail, so he had no idea who I was.

I initially decided to take the faceless author route because I wanted publishers and editors to see my writing, not my race. And it worked, so why fix what ain't broke? Back then the industry wasn't as open as it is nowadays for fresh new black voices, so I just used the voice that would get the most attention. If you asked the average mystery reader about me, they would emphatically tell you I was either a white male or female with an inside track on corporate America. They'd never guess I'm a black woman from Mississippi who was raised by an uneducated custodial worker in a three-bedroom house with four brothers and sisters. Yes, a black woman who so accurately describes a world she really knows nothing about, because no one wanted to know about the world she really knew.

Michael and I got married right out of college. He was a law student at Harvard and I just happened to be in Cambridge at a writers' retreat. I managed to pull away from the scholarly setting that epitomized the city for a quiet stroll in a nearby park. Michael was taking his lunch break in that same park. His red polo shirt and beige khakis were neatly pressed and fit to a "T." He didn't come across as my type, but that didn't stop me from looking. After a few minutes of trying to get this man to look my way, I made my move. I walked over and asked him if I could interview him for a writing-class exercise. He smiled and slid over to make room for me, my notebook, and a whole slew of loaded questions. Most of the things I asked him were genuinely for the exercise, but marital status and employer were not on the list. We talked for at least an hour before he glanced at his watch, made apologies, and started back toward one of those tall downtown buildings. Just as I made up my mind that this handsome smarty was not really interested in an up-and-coming author, he yelled back for my phone number.

I didn't do very well on the writing assignment, but I had dinner with Michael and one failed writing retreat turned into a budding relationship held together by a series of long-distance phone calls too expensive to mention. After a six-month courtship, Michael and I got engaged and within the same year we were married, and within weeks I found out I was pregnant.

I went from starving artist to law partner widow. During our short courtship, I didn't see Michael often, but I got the clear impression that he was extremely busy. After we were married, I learned that extremely busy actually meant chronic workaholic, type-A asshole. Michael quickly lost all his premarriage charm and before long I knew my place in the scheme of things. I didn't complain, since before I met Michael, I spent most of my waking hours trying to figure out where my next meal would come from or how I'd get my lights turned back on. He was rolling in cash and as much as I hated to admit it, I needed the money more than I needed the companionship. So that's how I got from Vicksburg, Mississippi to Melrose, Massachusetts.

I made my miserable marriage work for me by taking all the mundane drivel posing as conversation at those fancy-pants parties and turning them into a world I could get lost in. While my personal life took a downward spiral, my writing career soared.

Once I start on a new book, I get so caught up in the characters and all their mess, I almost feel like they're living through me. My life takes on whatever I'm writing about, at least when I'm sitting in front of my computer. I've even lashed out at my kids because they walked in and asked something just as one of my characters was chewing someone out. They would get a piece of that character before I could turn it off. And too many times Michael has caught me crying while writing late at night. One of my characters would be in the midst of an emotional moment and I'd get so caught up, I could feel their pain.

Thinking about Mabel's request was bringing me deeper into the reality of my own miserable existence. It meant thinking about home and all the misery I had left behind nearly eight years ago. Mabel is the only one of my siblings that I communicate with. She is the youngest of the girls and was always treated like the baby. That partly accounted for the reason she never got any kind of start in life. She didn't finish high school, got pregnant by some bum who never owned up to the child, and now she lived in the projects, surviving day by day off whatever someone would give her. I kept in touch with her mainly because I felt sorry for her. She didn't ask for that life, but after so many years, it was all she knew, so for her, it was one hand out after another.

Mabel was just over five feet tall and at least forty pounds overweight. She said it was baby fat from her pregnancy with her son Trey. But Trey was sixteen years old now. Mabel was homely if you just looked at her and didn't take the time to really study her features. In fact, she had a smile that would light up your day, but it was usually masked by the frustration of wondering where her next meal was gonna come from. The simplicity that was her very existence seems to give her a certain glow. Most people just said she was slow and looked confused all the time. I said it was the innocence of trying to see the best in people, even when there was no good to be seen.

Although Mabel could have been cuter on the surface, she did all the wrong things. There was nothing wrong with donning Wal-Mart specials, but Mabel never got clothes that fit her. Her blouses were always two sizes too big and she was always tugging at her polyester, elastic-in-the-waist pants. And her shoes were always a pair of run over black flats. Black goes with everything, so whether it was a pair of jeans and a sweater or a cute pink dress, Mabel would be sporting black flats. She had shoulder-length hair that always needed a perm and hadn't been able to hold a curl a single day in her life. She was the only one who even attempted to get the family together again. Every other conversation I had with her, she brought up getting all of us together for a big pig-pickin' or something. Mabel was right smack dab in the middle of five brothers and sisters, so she always had found security in being surrounded by her family. I guess that wouldn't be a bad thing, if her family had had the sense God gave them.

I have one other sister and two brothers. Grace is the oldest, then me, Mabel, Bobby and Andrew. I was the only sane one in the bunch and the only one who'd had the good sense to get the hell out of Mississippi while the gettin' was good. Mabel was destined to stay close to home for obvious reasons, but I never could figure out for the life of me why the other idiots didn't have a slight desire to see the rest of the world, or at least get out of Mississippi.

My oldest sister Grace was the mother hen. She thought that when Mama died, she was left in charge. And leave it to Mama, she probably told her some stupid shit like that just to make her feel needed. That was Grace's biggest problem. She needed to be needed. She lived from one crisis to the next. She'd never been married and any God-fearing man wouldn't dare get close to her. Grace is tall and lanky, probably 6'1" or more. Everyone always commented on how she could keep her weight under control so well, when she cooked so good. My guess was that it was all the crisis management she did for others. She barely had time to eat since she was always running to the side of whoever was ailing that week. Truth be told, Grace didn't need makeup. She was blessed with natural good looks, but no one had seen them because Maybelline had taken up permanent residence on her face. She had that old Southern woman makeup thing going. Too much black mascara gave her eyes a dead raccoon look and the red lipstick made her mouth look like a raging inferno. Add a hefty dose of blue eye shadow and you could just about say you'd seen my oldest sister firsthand. She was known around Vicksburg as the churchy diva—good looks and a nice body, but just enough religion to let the menfolk know they weren't getting any.

Mabel had told me that Grace was completely gray now and didn't do a thing to cover it up because someone once told her it made her look wise. I said it probably made her look real damn old. She was forty-three with no kids and no real life to speak of except the one she lived vicariously through everyone else around her. If the lady down the street had a child on his deathbed, it might as well have been Grace's child. She knew every detail of what the doctors had to say, what the family was going through and how much money they owed the hospital so far. As soon as she walked into a room, her head dropped as she prepared to spout out the latest misfortune to befall whichever unlucky soul she was living her life through that week.

Bobby was the one in the family that no one really wanted to talk about—or maybe that was me. Anyway, Bobby had been in and out of jail and in all likelihood he was either in or on his way back in. Smart boy, but he had never been able to put his head to anything long enough to make it come out right. He went to college for years, but never got anything close to a degree. Drinking and wild women were his main downfall. So much potential gone to waste. His good looks were the worst thing he could have inherited from Daddy. He is six feet tall and slim, but with muscles in all the places a man needs muscles. He got Daddy's good grade of hair and that pecan tan complexion that women can't seem to get enough of. Those deep-set dark brown eyes with the long black lashes were the kind that can look right through to the soul of a woman. Bobby only used them to look at butts and tits, and his women always had plenty of both. Women looked at him and thought someone that good-looking just couldn't be broke and no account. They soon found out. Bobby was full of charisma. He walked into a room and all eyes were on him. One smile could knock any unsuspecting woman off her horse. Several women claimed to have babies by him, but there was only one woman he claimed, and she had a house full of babies. Mabel told me they were up to four and she might be expecting again. I hadn't thought Bobby had been out of jail enough to father that many children.

As if the good looks weren't enough to give that boy trouble, he was cut and chiseled like a Roman god. All that time in jail would do that for a brother. When my daddy died, more women were at the funeral to see Bobby than to see my daddy laid to rest. There were at least three of his former girlfriends fighting over who was gonna serve the collards at the feeding after the funeral.

Last I had heard, he owed everybody in town, and the last time he went to jail was because somebody he had owed had ratted him out. Bobby had a way of getting money out of people. Even men got suckered by his charisma. He could come up with a lie so quickly you never would see it coming. He could be talking, smiling and all the while you were handing him money and didn't even realize it. Bobby learned a hard lesson with the money thing when those fools tried to kill him. You just couldn't mess with people's money. That was why I was making such a killing writing about corruption in corporate America. No matter how much money you had, you just didn't want it messed with.

Andrew was the last of the lot and the one who was still trying to figure out how he fit into the gang. Andrew was just a teenager when Mama and Daddy died. He barely even remembered the hard times in Mississippi. He only heard about them through our stories. By the time he was up to size, Daddy was real sick and Mama wasn't doing much better herself. All of us took care of him at some point in time, but he ended up living with Grace until he finished college. Grace was the perfect one to take him in. She had no children of her own, and Andrew was the perfect crisis for her. Flesh and blood, without a place to call home—Grace to the rescue.

The last time I saw Andrew, he was the typical high school kid with a bright future ahead of him. He was a shade or two darker than Bobby and carried a little more weight. He wasn't fat, just a little plumper around the middle. He was not as tall as Bobby either. Yes, of the two, Bobby certainly had gotten the looks, but Andrew had gotten the brains. He had graduated top of his class and was a successful accountant, according to Mabel. Andrew may not have had all the looks but he certainly had the Tayloe charm. He could flash those pretty white teeth, quote a line or two of Langston Hughes's "The Dream Keeper," and get anything he wanted. Mabel said every time they all got together, Andrew strutted in with his shirt and tie on like he thought he was somebody.

He was twenty-five now, and of all of us he had the best chance of ever getting beyond the ties of that stupid land Daddy had left to all of us. Andrew didn't know much about the land, so he didn't have much to say about it early on. He hadn't been around when Daddy slaved to get enough money to buy the land, let alone put a house on it. The house was long gone and the area around the land was being developed so quickly I was surprised the letter hadn't come sooner. It looked like progress to Andrew, but to the rest of us, it looked like the end. It was a welcome end to me, and a sad end to the rest. Yes, we would all be in better shape if we were in Andrew's shoes.

Too much thinking about the family was draining me even more and it was almost time to pick Junior up from camp. I needed to put in at least an hour or two in the cave. I glanced at that damn clock again; not yet noon, and my day was spinning in neutral. Too much was going on, and my ass was still glued to the mint green chaise with the solid pine frame and pleated skirt, another one of my more expensive and prized pieces. I got it because it looked like the perfect place to sit and read a book or have a cup of tea. I think Bessie spends more time curled up in it than I do.

I ventured back down into the cave, hoping that by sitting in front of my computer, a thought or two would jump onto the page. I'd been mulling over a couple of ideas for my next book, but nothing had played out properly in my head.

Here's the way it usually works for me. I get an idea for a book and then suddenly, without warning, the characters just start doing things in my head. Sometimes they start in my dreams and sometimes I'm just sitting there void of an intelligent thought and one of my characters will just start to talk and do things and I have to get away and write. Sounds strange, but how else could people who don't exist come to life on paper? I wished that one of them would do something so I could stop thinking about my crazy family.

I hadn't had any direct contact with my brothers and sisters, with the exception of Mabel, since Daddy died. I kept track of them through Mabel. I didn't have to ask—she would just give a report at the beginning of our conversation. For example:

"Hey sis, dis Mabel."

"Mabel, it's good to hear from you. How are things?"

"Can't complain on dis end. How de chiren doin'?"

"Lisa and Junior are fine, doing well in school and, well, just being teenagers."

"You know my boy ain't doin' so well in school. That boy won listen to nobody to save his life. He say he gone drop out soon as he fine a job."

"Well, I'm sorry to hear that."

"And Grace say that Lancaster woman down the road from her ain't got no better—in fact she worse. You know soon as they cut on that cancer it spread like wildfire. Same thing happen to Daddy, you know."

There was no point in explaining to her that that's not what happened with Daddy or the Lancaster woman. So I let her go on.

"Andrew met a girl and dey say he in luv. I thank she cute, but Grace say she just afta his money. I didn' know he had no money myself. Yo husman still doin' good at his job?"

"Yes, things are going well for Michael. He likes the firm and work seems to keep pouring in, so he keeps busy."

"Bobby goin' back to jail dey say. I ain't seen him, but Grace say he called her one night late sayin' he needed her to bail him out. He say he didn' do nuthin', but dats what he always say. Lord, dat boy done spend his whole life hine bars."

"Mabel, Mabel, honey, someone's at the door and I have to see who it is. Michael is expecting an important package. I'll call you later. Gotta run. Love you, bye now."

I usually switch the lie each time she calls in order to keep her off my track. One time it's the doorbell, the next time it's a call on our second line, which we don't even have. One time when the kids were here, I had Junior scream like he had hurt himself so I could get off the phone with Mabel. He enjoyed the little game and I saw no harm in amusing him while accomplishing my own selfish goal. I never call Mabel back and I never have to since she always makes a point to try to contact me at least once a month. A few years back I tried to reach her when I got news that Bobby had been shot and might be dead. But Mabel doesn't have her own phone and whichever neighbor's number she had given me last didn't feel like walking over to her house to get her, so they just told me I had the wrong number.

Turns out Bobby hadn't been shot. Some fool he was hanging out with had been shot. Either way, the nosey-ass person who called me all the way from Mississippi was just trying to get a rise out of me. Most of the folk in Vicksburg know where I live and speculate about the situation with my family. Periodically I get a call from some concerned bystander wanting me to know how my family is doing. I live most of my days not even thinking about those fools, but it did trouble me to hear that Bobby had been shot.

So maybe on some level they still matter to me, but they'll never get the pleasure of knowing that.

I decided to call Mabel this time. She shouldn't be the only one dealing with this mess about the land. My selfish brothers and sisters were in Mississippi avoiding the issue and I wasn't doing any better by isolating myself in Massachusetts. I'd be an adult and make the first move. As Daddy always said, "It takes one to know one." For eight years I had been acting as foolishly as they had, but avoiding the issue had to stop. It wasn't what I was looking for, but the diversion of dealing with my family would take my mind off my failing marriage. I picked up the phone and surprised myself by dialing the number from memory. It had been years since I'd dialed that number.

Chapter 4

I talked to Mabel and got the number for the man who'd called her about the land. After getting the runaround for nearly an hour, I finally talked to someone who sounded remotely intelligent. Within an hour, I'd talked to three different people and finally got a clear understanding of what was going on. In a nutshell, the Vicksburg-Warren County Economic Development Foundation was trying to "establish and maintain a program of economic development that will enhance industry's potential for growth and profit and make the community attractive to new industry," as Mr. Spencer so eloquently explained. It just meant that they were trying to keep up with the times and attract new business so the city could make more money. They were interested in our land because it sits right in the middle of the new area targeted for growth. They needed to extend a road in the area to accommodate all the growth around our land, and my silly siblings were standing in the way. Common sense said that if you throw up a shopping mall and several apartment complexes and other little odds and ends, you were bound to need to provide a decent road to give people access to the area. It made sense to me, but then again, I lived in Massachusetts and not the backwoods of Mississippi.

According to Mr. Spencer, he had talked to one of my brothers and gotten the impression we had no intention of selling the land. I knew right away he couldn't be talking about Andrew, so it had to be the convicted felon Bobby. I had no idea how to locate Bobby to find out what the hell he was thinking, which meant I'd eventually have to talk to my sister Grace. This was not going in the right direction and still not a word on paper for my novel. I needed another drink before making a call to Mississippi.

Drinking a glass or two here and there was how it had started. I hated to admit my drinking had gotten out of hand. My seventeen years of wedded bliss had been nothing more than night after lonely night waiting for Michael to get home. On the nights he did come home on time, we would rush off to those stuffy cocktail parties or thousand-dollar-plate benefits. Who pays a thousand dollars for a plate of chicken, rice, and green beans? We'd certainly done our share of it. I should have figured it out when, the day after we returned home from our honeymoon, Michael rushed off to Portland, Oregon, to handle some high-profile case. We had only been married a week, and there I was in that tiny one-bedroom condominium in Cambridge all alone.

That first week alone turned into months and before I knew it, I had adjusted to being married and living like a single person. I was pregnant with Lisa, but I went to all the doctor's appointments by myself. Seeing that tiny baby swimming around on the ultrasound machine just wasn't the same experiencing it alone. After Lisa was born, Michael swore he would slow down. But then they made him a partner. The word "slow" was permanently removed from his vocabulary, and that really worked my nerve in the bedroom. While Michael spent twelve to fourteen hours a day at the office, I spent my days taking care of Lisa and trying my best to write a book someone would actually want to read. The more I got shut out of Michael's world, the more I created a world of my own. And in no time, the best-selling novels started rolling off the presses.

The drinking got worse after Junior was born—two children and still no husband in sight. I was a successful author, but no one knew it because I was using my pen name, which meant no major book signings with adoring fans pouring in to sit at the feet of their favorite author. My nights were spent with my computer and a bottle of Dom Perignon. After I got the babies to bed, confident that Michael would not be home before midnight, I spent hours drinking and writing. Those two things became my passion. With the liquor swirling in my head, the ideas were free to flow with little to no apprehension. Good guys and bad guys leaped off the page and did stuff great novels are made of. So now, after seventeen years, ten best-sellers and more money than you can shake a stick at, I was a lonely drunk who was scared to call her judgmental sister in Mississippi.

I have a wine cellar downstairs in the cave. It's a small cellar, just enough room for the good stuff. When I converted the damp, musty hellhole into my writing area, there was one room that likely had been a bathroom or laundry room. It became my cellar. After walking through, looking at bottles of Moet White Star, Cakebread chardonnay, and sauvignon blanc, I realized this moment was not worthy of the good stuff. Family problems plus writer's block equaled cheap supermarket wine. I went back upstairs, pulled a bottle of Beringer's Founders' Estate from the kitchen cabinet, and in no time the mellowing effect was kicking in.

After several glasses of wine, I was ready to make the call, or so I thought. When I got up to reach for the phone, I almost fell over. I grabbed the edge of the couch and steadied myself. I lay down, hoping to stop the room from spinning. I told myself that I'd been stressing over the novel and the call to Mabel so much, I'd worn myself out. As I drifted off to sleep, I let my mind go back to an earlier time in Mississippi, a time when life was not so complicated and not so easy at the same time.

The year was 1971 when Daddy first started talking about buying some land and building us a house. We had been renting from the Dobbs family all my life, and their three-bedroom ranch-style house seemed like it was ours. Daddy talked about our own home day and night. He'd get up early in the morning and, before he went off to work, he'd make sure all of us knew we would not be living on top of each other in that little house forever. He'd come home at night and tell us what he'd accomplished that day. If he'd been to the bank, he'd talk about that. If he'd looked at a plot of land, he'd talk about how great it looked and how we'd all just love it. Some days there wouldn't be anything to report, but on those days Daddy would just dream out loud. He'd talk about the layout of the house and how we'd all get our own bed and have so much more space because the house would have at least five bedrooms—big bedrooms with room enough for a couple of beds and dressers and all our clothes. He talked about it so much and for long that when it finally started happening, we could hardly sit still.

Sure enough, we bought the land. It was a beautiful plot of land just like Daddy said. Fifteen acres of flat land with nothing on it but possibilities. He'd take us out there every Sunday after church to see what had happened the week before. I remember when they first started breaking up the land, there were big machines everywhere. I just knew we were important. Who would send out machines that big to do work for just regular old people?

"They send out anything you want as long as yo' money is green," Daddy chuckled.

I had no idea it took so much to build a house. They laid the foundation and that seemed to take forever. We went back several Sundays in a row and nothing but more foundation work had been accomplished, nothing that looked remotely like a house. Daddy used that opportunity to preach to us about the importance of a good foundation. He quoted the Bible and added his own little made-up parts to make his lesson interesting. We didn't want our mansion to be built on a shabby foundation, so four youngsters took a newfound interest in concrete, studs, and a bunch of other stuff we had never heard of.

When Michael and I bought our first house, I can remember quoting some of Daddy's words when the men started talking about the foundation. Michael thought I had lost it.

"You sound like some Southern Baptist preacher, Bev," he joked.

"Yeah, I may sound like a preacher, but if that foundation isn't sound, I'm gonna sound like everything but a preacher," I fired back, as he walked off shaking his head.

Those days of building that house were actually the first time I had ever paid a lot of attention to my daddy. Sure, I played with him when I was little and all that, but building that house was bringing out a side of him I'd never seen. Daddy had always been the soft-spoken one between my parents. My mother was the straightforward type. But Daddy did everything to make things more pleasant for the people around him.

"Johnston, that's why folks call you—'cause they know you just crazy enough to get out of your bed and come," Mama yelled at 3:00 in the morning, when Daddy was on his way to get old man Daniel out of the ditch again.

Old man Daniel was Daddy's second cousin, but to everyone else he was just the town drunk. Daniel wasted all his money on hard liquor and spent too many nights falling into ditches trying to get home. He wandered up and down the road mumbling to himself and pulling imaginary stuff out of his pockets, until someone got pissed enough to call Daddy to come get him. That particular night he had wandered into the white folks' neighborhood and ended up in one of their clean, well-trimmed ditches. The phone rang and woke up everybody in the house. Daddy answered and started to grab clothes before he even hung up the phone. Mama sat up in the bed shaking her head.

"It's that fool again, ain't it? What he do this time? Please tell me he dead, so at least I know we won't get no more calls like this in the middle of the night. And you goin' right out there and get him again. How he gon ever learn, Johnston, as long as he got you?" she continued, almost out of breath.

"That's right, long as he got me. You know I'm all he got," Daddy replied to let Mama know she was fighting a losing battle.

Daddy went to Daniel's rescue that night like he had so many times previously. We all sat around Mama on their king-size bed, waiting for Daddy to get back. That night ended like so many others had: Daddy back at home, Daniel safe in his bed, and Mama still pouting about her crazy husband letting another lowlife use him. No more than two weeks later, Daniel used the last of his nine lives. He drunkenly wandered into the night trying to get home and was hit by a motorist not expecting to see an old drunk lying in the middle of the road at 2:00 in the morning. Daniel was killed on the spot and, of course, Daddy got the call.

My daddy was nearly 6'2" and rang in at about 270 pounds—a big black man with hands that covered your behind something fierce when he was giving you a spanking. He was light-skinned with nice curly black hair. Some say he got that light skin and good hair because he was one of them babies grandmother had by the white man she worked for. Daddy never talked about his ancestry and it never really mattered because he was the length and breadth of the Tayloe family. Most black Southern families were primarily matriarchal. The mamas ran the house and made all the minor decisions and the daddies were not around in most cases. But the Tayloe house was different. My daddy was always there and always in charge. Even though my mama had all the mouth in the house, we all knew Daddy ran the show. Mama could talk until she was blue in the face, as she did most of the time—but we all knew that when it came final decision time, Johnston Tayloe wore the pants.

I remember finally moving into that new house we had worked on for nearly a year. In fact, Grace and I had moved in before the house was done. We packed blankets, pillows, and a change of clothes, and spent many nights sleeping on the bare floors in our empty five-bedroom mansion. Mama and Daddy didn't try to stop us. Our enthusiasm was contagious and soon they let Mabel join us. Mama and Daddy tried to maintain some dignity by waiting until the house was complete and had all the furniture before they started spending the night.

On moving day, us girls fought tirelessly with Bobby about which room would be ours. We wanted the one that had its own bathroom close by, since girls tend to need the facilities a good deal more often than boys. We won the battle, and after a week in the house Bobby was glad he didn't get that room. Someone was always in that bathroom. The toilet flushing and water running made it impossible to sleep or study or get a moment of privacy.

There were three bathrooms in the house: one downstairs for company; one in Mama and Daddy's room that was off-limits to all kids, except in the case of a parent-approved emergency; and the other bathroom was right beside the girls' room. We had to share the bathroom with Bobby, but it was still our bathroom. Mama and Daddy got their own room and the girls and Bobby each got a room. There was a small room next to Mama and Daddy's that was the sewing room, but had already been appointed to Grace when she reached the age when girls need their own space. I had no idea what that was about and I was glad I wasn't going to be in the room by myself. That big house was kind of frightening at night. The last bedroom was the nursery and with our parents' track record, it would be put to good use very soon.

Within no time we were moving around in that big house just like we had always been living there. Mama announced she was planting a huge garden in the back and all of us kids sighed because we knew that meant pulling weeds and all kinds of other outdoor activity we weren't too fond of. Mama was always starting some new project, which simply meant we kids would be getting another chore added to our list. Mama was the opposite of Daddy. She rarely had kind words for anyone. She was 5'5" and as round as she was tall. She spent most of her time barking out tasks for us and complaining about Daddy working too hard. They were a strange pair, but we never doubted their love for one another. How could she not love Daddy? He was fine as the day was long and just as nice as any man could be. Mama was his backbone. She would say the things Daddy never had the nerve to say. He'd look at her sometimes and say, "Martha, you ain't got to be so ugly about it," when Mama was ranting and raving about a bunch of nothing. But that was Mama—she'd call a spade a spade, everybody from Daddy's drunk cousin to the sorry skirt-tail-chasing preacher she wished the church would get rid of.

"That man ain't right, Johnston. You oughta see the way he look at Grace. I need to clean his eyeballs out with lye soap. Preacher man ain't supposed to be lustin' so bad. He spose to be helpin' other folk get rid of they lustin', but he can't keep his eyes off my baby girl hind parts. Nasty nigger," she added.

35

Most of the time Daddy just laughed at her, knowing full well she was right. But he would never have the nerve to say stuff like that about the preacher man. Daddy was one of the deacons and they knew exactly what the good Reverend was up to, but then again, most of the deacons were up to the same thing, so why bother?

After a few days in the new house, despite all our fixing this and moving that, our furniture still looked like doll furniture. Nothing was quite grand enough. It was so much old surrounded by so much new. We dealt with it just the same, since Daddy said it took everything we had just to get the land and build the house. The furniture and nice pictures for the walls would come later. We had been cramped in that three-bedroom rental for so long, this felt like too much room. All three girls were still in a room together, but at least there were other rooms to go to when you weren't sleeping or getting dressed. There was the den, or family room as we called it. The living room was off-limits to all the kids. It was where Mama and Miss Flossie went to gossip. Mama said it would also serve as the courting room as soon as Grace was old enough to take company. Little did Mama know, Grace was already taking plenty of company, just not at the house.

After the first year in the house, we were finally settled in and it was like old business. Bobby thought it was his job to pick on each of the girls and we spent most of our time trying to figure out how to get him back. Daddy worked hard as usual, so he was rarely around to even enjoy what he had worked so hard for. Mama was acting strange most days, talking to herself and forgetting where she put stuff. Grace predicted she was pregnant because she had seen Mama like this before. And sure enough, she was. Not a year and a week after we were in the new house, Mama announced she was having another little bundle of joy. Country folk sure do know how to make some babies. Just when you think they have no more room or money for another head, they pop out another baby. Daddy strutted around the house like a proud rooster, watching Mama's belly grow each day. You'd think he might be worried about trying to feed another mouth, but with four already, what's one more hand snatching at the pile?

In no time, the Tayloe family fit nicely into our two-story, five-bedroom home just off the Mississippi River in Vicksburg. On a good day, you could stand at my parents' bedroom window and see all up and down the river. Folks all over Mississippi called it "Ole Man River" because it has long played a part in the historical, economic, and residential development of Vicksburg. Since the early 1800s, the Mississippi had been the lifeline of my hometown, but for the Tayloe family it was our piece of paradise—our own river, practically in our backyard. When the crews were clearing the land to build our house, Daddy asked them to leave one tree that was so big its roots ran all the way to the banks of the river. That tree was our refuge point on many a hot summer afternoon. It was a great spot for a picnic or just to sit back and sip lemonade and watch the riverboats sail by. Daddy referred to it as our "tree planted by the river," as if he had put it there himself, hundreds of years ago, just for the Tayloe family to enjoy.

I jumped up from the couch and grabbed the ringing phone, sure I had missed some important deadline.

"Two o'clock, damn. I was supposed to pick Junior up at one-thirty," I mumbled as I put the receiver to my mouth.

"Hello? Yes, this is she. Yes, I'm on my way. I had an emergency, something I had to take care of and I'm on my way out the door right now," I lied, and threw the phone down before the coach could ask me anything else.

In no time, I had picked up both Lisa and Junior, grabbed food at the drive-through and was back at home by 3:00 with two mouthy teenagers gobbling down Burger King burgers and fries. Junior ran straight to the den and turned on the television. I watched him and Lisa flop down on the sofa like two zombies with eyes glued to angry rappers shouting for people to "move, get out the way."

It was time to face the music myself. I had to call one of those idiots and I would probably end up in Mississippi before the week was out.

They may be getting me back to Vicksburg, but there is no way in hell they'll lull me back into their backward way of doing things. I say sell the damn land to the highest bidder, and keep stepping forward. All their trips down memory lane will not get me to change my mind. I picked up the phone and dialed Grace's number.

Chapter 5

"Hi, Jake, this is Bev. I have more bad news." I paused for him to cuss and scream.

They needed an outline and something that remotely resembled a book in progress. My publishing company had just signed me for another four-book deal. They paid me a healthy up-front fee and now they were eagerly awaiting some sign of life from me.

"Oh, Bev, why the hell do you keep doing this to me? What do you think I am, some kind of magician? I can't make the deadlines disappear into thin air. I need something, anything. Just an outline will do. I have a meeting in ten minutes and you're on my list of things to discuss. They're all waiting to see what crazy wonderful things you have for our readers this time," he went on.

He was just blowing smoke up my ass. But that was okay. He got paid good money to keep me happy.

"Okay, Jake, let me be honest with you. I don't really have anything brewing right this minute." I could hear the panic in his breathing. "But I promise I will not disappoint. Don't I always come through?"

"Bev, Paul just motioned for me—the meeting is about to start. Listen, what I'll do is grab that crazy-ass outline you sent me two years ago. You remember, the one about the futuristic robot?" he said, laughing.

Two years ago, I had been in a similar predicament and sent Jake a really far-out pitch about a robot, and I don't even remember all the details. I knew it wouldn't fly when I took five minutes to send it to him in a last-minute e-mail.

"I'll pitch that today and of course everyone will get a laugh, then I'll let them know you're working on the real deal and will get it to me by Friday. Right, Bev? No later than Friday. My job is on the line at that point."

I knew he wasn't bullshitting. Friday would be about as much stalling as I could do. Surely I would be able to come up with something by Friday.

"Yes, Jake, Friday. I have a family emergency and I'm heading out to Mississippi today, but I'll e-mail you something as soon as I get settled."

"Is everything okay? I mean, with the family—yes, Paul, I'm on my way—Who lives in Mississippi, anyway?"

"Can't talk about it—just be assured I'll get you what you need in plenty of time for you to do your song and dance you do so well. Thanks again, Jake," I said as I hung up the phone.

When Michael got home from work, I explained the situation while throwing some things into a suitcase and trying desperately to make reservations at my favorite bed-and-breakfast in Vicksburg.

"Bev, do you have to drive? It'll take you a day and a half to get there if you make absolutely no stops. You know, that's what they make planes for."

Michael went on questioning my need to drive and I gave him a half answer as I continued pecking away at the keys to confirm my arrival time at the Cedar Grove Inn. I hadn't visited the inn in years, so I was sure to book the best suite they had available. I wanted to make this dreaded trip as bearable as possible and a couple of nights at Cedar Grove would help.

"At least take the kids along for company. I really don't like the idea of you on the road for so long alone. It's settled—you're taking the kids."

I just looked up at Michael occasionally to acknowledge his yapping, but kept at my work of making reservations and packing. Against my better judgment, I agreed that the trip might be good for the kids. They hadn't seen their family in eight years and as much as I tried to tell myself they were content with that, I knew they wanted some connection to that part of the family.

When they were younger, we visited Mississippi at least a couple of times a year, usually during the summer, which should have been a crime because of the heat. No one should have to spend a summer in the South unless they are a glutton for punishment. Even still, every summer we made the long drive to spend a week with the family. Lisa is old enough to remember those times very well, but Junior is pretty vague in his discussion of the hot summer nights sitting on Aunt Grace's porch drinking lemonade and swatting mosquitoes.

"Ma, do I have to?" both Lisa and Junior chimed in unison.

"Yes, you have to go. Didn't you hear your father? Besides, the trip will be good for you. All either of you do is walk around with that phone stuck to the side of your head. Both of you need a change of scenery."

"But, Ma, what about camp?"

"Look, boy, you only have three more days anyway. If you don't know it by now, you ain't gonna learn it in three days."

I hated forcing them to come along. They both already had their plans for the week, and ninety-degree Southern heat was not part of it. I appealed to Lisa's desire to hook up with her cousin Trey, and Junior was sold when I mentioned that he would be the man in charge during the trip and we might even get to see the National Military Park where his granddaddy worked when I was his age. I finished last-minute preparations and started loading the truck, while Lisa and Junior grabbed things they just had to take to Mississippi. Neither of them had been to Mississippi in eight years, so I don't know what they "just had to take."

Lisa walked around gathering those little miniskirts and shorty shorts she knew I hated. She did look good in them, I had to admit. She had that perfect sixteen-year-old figure, just right for your senior year in high school and preparing for the college boys. I remember those days—I wasn't fortunate enough to have the figure, but I remember the excitement just the same. I was at least fifteen pounds overweight as a teenager, so I didn't get to go out with the cutest boys. I got the smart ones, the ones the popular girls just laughed at. My sister Grace had been so slender and pretty, most people were shocked to find out we were related. When Grace introduced me as her younger sister, they just looked at me like I was from Mars or something. Back then, I hated the fact that I got the secondhand guys. The jocks all wanted the cheerleader type, not the editor of the school newspaper. The teenage boys were looking at the girls with the latest hairstyles and nice clothes, and of course the girls who had started filling out already. Grace was slim, but she got her boobs early and the boys were right there trying to get their hands on them. I don't think I got boobs until I was pregnant with Lisa. Fortunately, after the engorgement and breast-feeding, I was left with a little cleavage to make my formal gowns hang better.

I envied Grace back then, but I think it all turned out just fine in the end. I got the bookworm for a husband. Michael wouldn't know what to do with a football. He knows his stuff in court and that's what matters when the pep rallies and Friday night football games are over.

Sometimes I can't even believe I have a sixteen-year-old child, nearly six feet tall and with curves in "all the wrong places," as her daddy would say. She got her height from my side of the family since not one female Lamark was much more than 5'5". She was wearing her hair in one of those short sassy cuts that shows a little too much neck if you asked me. My daddy always said, "You don't need to see too much of a woman's neck—too seductive." I never really figured out why Daddy really disapproved of showing off the neck, but I didn't like it because it made her look way too mature and sophisticated. I watched her pack a pair of those hip-hugger jeans. She had a smile on her face that let me know she knew exactly what those jeans were for. A black woman with some booty knows what a pair of those jeans will do to a man. I hated the fact that Lisa knew, too, and I had no idea how much she knew. I remembered she was probably still wearing my thong underwear.

I had given her the standard boys, sex, birth control talk, but she'd acted like it was just information and nothing else. That concerned me. She didn't act like the typical little hot-behind teenager, but it's those quiet ones you have to watch most of the time. I remember my junior year in high school, the quietest girl in our class ended up pregnant. Apparently she didn't talk, but she must've done something, because before senior year, she had a baby.

Junior, on the other hand, was at that stage where he had interest in girls, but wasn't sure how to handle it. I caught him a time or two trying to look up stuff on the Internet. I found one of those girlie magazines in his room and, of course, I've had to change his sheets more often since he seemed to be spilling his manhood at night. His voice was starting to crack a little as the little-boy highs tried to grab on to the base sounds. It was all part of growing up. Raising teenagers was taking me to a new level in the motherhood department.

Junior was almost a cookie-cutter image of his father: a shorty for his age, thin enough to still look like a grade schooler instead of a junior high man. His complexion was a nice pecan tan with enough light brown in his hair to let you know there was some mixed ancestry going on somewhere a generation or two ago. He had the typical Lamark build—small frame, mostly muscle, very little fat. No matter what they eat, I swear the Lamarks don't gain a pound. Junior had inherited that gene. He can put away some food, but you'd never know it just by looking at him.

Within a matter of hours, my two children and I were throwing almost-forgotten necessities into the truck, desperate to get on the road before it got too late. But that didn't stop Michael from running his mouth.

"Bev, you really need to get going if you plan to drive most of the night. You really should try to make it to Baltimore before you have to stop. Remember, only stops in major metropolitan areas—none of that pulling-off-God-knows-where stuff."

Where did he think we were going? Mississippi *is* God knows where. I promised to follow all of his rules, knowing full well I would do what I damn well pleased. I hated it when Michael got into one of his "I'm the man of the house" speeches. Lisa and Junior sat impatiently waiting in the truck as I blew Michael a kiss, threw my purse on the floor beneath Junior's feet, and started my journey.

As we drove off, Michael stood in the driveway, with Bessie purring and slithering around his ankles. I had left him instructions for getting her boarded while we were gone. The two looked like a lonesome pair, but they'd make do. Besides, this trip was necessary—not pleasant, but necessary.

Junior, Lisa, and I rounded the curve leading out of our neighborhood. The streets were almost clear with the exception of a few old folks strolling along enjoying the warm afternoon. We passed a few people we knew. I waved; the kids just kept looking ahead as if there was nothing ahead of us but a roadway of excitement. That's one of the things I hate about our neighborhood. No one knows his neighbor and no one seems to mind. We all did our own thing and went our own way and only spoke if we made eye contact with another before either could look away quickly enough. There was no sense of community like in Mississippi. As we made our way out of the city and headed south, the kids kept their blank stare and I kept my mind on the highway. With so much traffic going in all directions, I dodged and ducked in and out of cars, sport-utility vehicles, and minivans. As I meandered my way through the tangled mess, I couldn't help but think of my last trip back home.

We had only been back in Melrose a week since visiting Daddy in Vicksburg. Grace had called with the latest diagnosis and as soon as I heard the words "days numbered," I pleaded with Michael to take me to be by his bedside. I couldn't bear the thought of not being near Daddy during the fight of his life. He had been diagnosed with lung cancer and the doctors weren't sure if surgery would make a difference or not. Grace had been going back and forth on the decision, but as Daddy grew weaker, we all agreed he deserved the chance. The surgery was scheduled for 8:00 AM Wednesday morning and I spent most of Tuesday afternoon trying to get a flight.

When I finally got a flight, within minutes all planes were grounded due to a snowstorm. Michael and I paced the airport waiting area as if our frequent steps would melt the snow and make the planes take off again. We paced all night and at last, at 4:00 AM, there was a break in the weather pattern and the planes were allowed to resume operation. It took another two hours to get the planes and the runway cleared enough for takeoff, but by 7:00 AM we were in the air, headed for Vicksburg. Daddy went into surgery that morning, just as scheduled. They put him under at 8:30, as Michael and I were sailing over Mississippi about to land. As soon as the plane landed, I called the hospital to let them know I was en route, and I heard the words that still ring in my ear today. "Mr. Tayloe didn't make it." He never made it through surgery. My daddy was dead and I was standing in the middle of an airport terminal wondering what to do next.

Somehow it got stuck in my mind that boarding a plane had something to do with my daddy's death. I hadn't flown since that day.

As we drove along the interstate, Lisa and Junior were into their own thing. As for me, my thoughts were all over the place. After eight years, this trip had an all too familiar sting to it: going to Mississippi to bury my daddy eight years ago, and today going to Mississippi to sell off the one thing on this earth that still had his name on it. I glanced at Lisa and Junior as I wiped the tear from my cheek, swearing that this was best for all of us. Getting rid of that land that no one knew what to do with would finally end the misery.

Before setting out on this gruesome journey, I'd talked to Grace after hitting nothing but dead ends trying to reach Bobby. I hated to dial her number, but I had to talk to someone with half-good sense. And that was about all Grace had: half. While we were talking, I knew she had a napkin in her bony little hand, wiping the phone as if germs were waiting to jump into her mouth. That's her habit and I've hated it since we were teenagers. Grace wouldn't even pick up the phone until she had something in her hand to wipe it off with. In desperate times, she'd just use her shirtsleeve.

She had insisted that I stay with her, but the trip itself was enough torture. I couldn't put myself through two nights under the same roof with Grace, getting her version of the obituary page, and watching her wipe the phone like a maniac. I let her know that we had a two-bedroom suite booked at the Cedar Inn so we wouldn't inconvenience anyone. I made up some lie and blamed my rooming decision on the kids.

"You know how kids are, Grace," I said, giggling.

She bought the lie, although, truth be known, Lisa and Junior would love to spend the night camped out at Aunt Grace's, listening to anything that fell from her skinny little lips. There was no one like Grace in Melrose. There was no one like most of my family in Melrose. The kids loved listening to the Southern drawl that made their sentences go on forever. That's almost the only thing Junior seems to remember about my family.

Grace had ended the conversation by again mentioning that we could simply stay with her and save some money, unless we had so much we just didn't know what to do with all of it. That was her way of throwing off on my lifestyle and my husband. My family has never really understood what I do. Most families would be proud that their sister is a best-selling author, but my folks just complain about all those white-folk stories and why I don't use my real name. I considered telling them the real reason I use a pen name, but they are confident that I do it because I am ashamed of them. Most days, that's not too far from the truth.

46

My family also has a problem with my husband and his career. Michael is Haitian, although he's spent most of his life right here in the States. He was born in Haiti and lived there for at most five years before his parents moved to Buffalo, New York. Going from Haiti to Buffalo? Who knows what they were thinking, but that's where they still are today. Michael has a few customs that are different from the typical Southern Mississippi household, and he has taken more than his share of ribbing from my folks.

"Why you marry that high-minded lawyer man anyway?" Mabel once asked.

I ignored her and just passed it off as babbling from my confused younger sister, until I found out the rest of them felt the same way.

"You so money-hungry, a good American black man ain't good enough for you. Black men know how to make money too," Bobby added, without two dimes to rub together himself.

After a few years of marriage, I stopped defending my life mate to my family. I wanted them to accept Michael, and I bent over backward to help the two different cultures mesh. Michael was accustomed to doing things a certain way, and my family just seemed to get rubbed the wrong way by it time and time again. For example, in Michael's culture, you brought a gift when you visited someone, even family. Whenever you were traveling from out of town, visiting someone you didn't see often, you brought something— not something grand or expensive, but something. If it was a dinner, he'd bring the wine or a centerpiece for the table. If it was just a visit, he'd bring the lady of the house flowers, and the man, cigars or whatever he was into. This was just Michael's custom. Well, my family made a big deal out of that one. They said he was just trying to act like he was better than them and was showing off how much money he had. He would always try to take something nice for my family since, of course, they were family, but the nicer the gift, the harder they criticized him.

When we went down for Trey's championship baseball game ten years ago, Michael wanted to take us all out to dinner afterward to celebrate. He wanted to go someplace nice to show Trey that life isn't just burgers and fries. He went all out. He booked reservations at an upscale French restaurant and even reserved a limousine to carry all of us. When the long black super stretch limo pulled up to Grace's front door, they started to mumble something under their breath. The ride in the limo was so bad you could cut the tension with a knife. Michael was confused. Bobby and Grace made comments about throwing away money and how no one was impressed with all that waste. That was the trip that did it for Michael. After that, he stopped making trips home with me. I traveled with the kids or alone and I always made up a nice excuse for his absence. I had no trouble convincing them he was too busy or working with an important client, because they probably didn't care to see him anyway.

Too many times I had wanted to talk to Grace about my marriage, but I didn't want her to automatically jump on Michael's case. They already had enough negative feelings—I wasn't going to add to it by letting her know my marriage was less than perfect. Besides, I got a little pleasure from seeing the envy in her eyes whenever we visited.

After nearly two hours of daydreaming, I realized Junior had popped in a CD of one of those boy bands they love so much. They all sound alike to me—just a bunch of white boys trying too hard to have some soul. Junior had no idea what real soul was. Real soul music was back in my day when voices like Marvin Gaye hit the scene. That was real singing. This boy band could learn a thing or two from Marvin Gaye or Teddy Pendergrass. Ohh, Teddy Pendergrass—now that was some real singing. Anytime a man can sing and make a woman throw her panties on the stage, you know he's singing.

Junior bopped his head and sang along to the lyrics, singing, "Bye, Bye, Bye," right along with the group. Lisa sat in the back, flipping through her latest magazine, no doubt checking out the handsome boys with no shirts and their pants halfway down their behinds. Lisa, boys, and sex—that was a thought I wasn't ready for, so I put my attention back on the road.

After another hour of travel, Junior was ready to stop for a bathroom break. I had expected it the minute we left Melrose. That was the way it had worked for all our trips in the past. I don't care how old they are, children will never go to the bathroom like you tell them to before a long trip. The story is always the same: "Ma, I didn't have to go before we left home, honest," he would mumble while squirming in his seat like he had a fire burning in his shorts.

This time he had done great. After seven hours of driving, we were in the Baltimore area. We looked for an exit with decent food and decided to make it a bathroom/food stop. While Junior dashed to the restroom, Lisa and I scanned the menu at the Cracker Barrel counter, trying to decide if we'd order food to go or just sit down and eat. Just then a man walked out of the restroom area, sucking his teeth and maneuvering a toothpick around his mouth like he was trying to perform an extraction rather than pick his teeth. His belly was lapping over what looked like either a belt or a thin string of rubber tubing. He had grease stains on the front of his shirt that he likely didn't see because of the protruding belly. The cashier was trying to be professional and not draw any attention to the man, but I couldn't seem to look away from him. He was wearing a pair of dress pants, dress shoes and white tube socks.

I tried not to make eye contact with Lisa. The teeth sucking was enough to send her over the edge, but his apparel would be too much for my official member of the fashion police. When the man was out of my immediate line of sight, I turned to look at Lisa. Suprisingly, she was trying to be adult about it and put her attention back on the menu. We both stared at the list of dinner entrees and tasty breakfast options, but my mind was still on Mr. GQ, who had pushed the door open to leave. Just as he thought he was out of earshot, he let one rip. With that, Lisa bent over, doubled with laughter, and I wasn't far behind her. Junior came out of the bathroom to find the two of us stumbling around the Cracker Barrel waiting area, laughing like hyenas.

"Ma, Lisa, what in the world? Everybody's staring at you."

"At us? Well, they didn't see or hear what we just saw," I said. We both laughed louder.

We asked the cashier to show us to a table. Junior just had to hear about this guy. This was going to be a sit-down meal for sure. There was no way I could drive along listening to Lisa describe the scene to Junior. We were already in Baltimore, it wasn't late, so we got a table, ordered breakfast, lunch, and dinner meals and laughed our behinds off about Mr. Etiquette.

After the meal, I was still full of energy, so I decided to drive on at least a few more hours before stopping for the night. Michael had suggested Baltimore, but my adrenaline was pumping and I needed to take advantage of the energy burst. The kids talked about everything from whether Halle Barry was really having sex with that man, to the latest Jay-Z video. I didn't know Halle Barry had a new movie out, and to my surprise, it wasn't even new anymore. That was now on my list of things to do when I got back to Melrose. The kids kept running their mouths and I watched for exits as I entered the Virginia area. I was hoping to make it to North Carolina before stopping for the night, but that would not be so.

Why I let those kids drink so much is beyond me. After only another hour and a half, Junior was squirming in his seat again. I lectured about drinking all that soda as if it were going to negate the fact that I had to pull over yet again and let this child empty his bladder.

"But, Ma, all I had was one drink with my food, and I don't just have to pee."

"I have half a mind to just keep driving and let you learn your lesson, young man."

Lisa was nodding in the back, ignoring my lecture on proper

travel etiquette. She had heard the speech one time too many and, after sixteen years, finally had the good sense to limit her beverage intake so we wouldn't have to stop so damn much. I continued mumbling under my breath as I pulled off the first exit ramp I found.

Chapter 6

This time I didn't care if we found a decent place or not. I knew I was somewhere in Virginia, but I didn't bother to look at the exit number. We had just passed Petersburg a few miles back, so I wasn't sure when we'd get to the next major city. A gas station would do just fine for Junior. *Besides, he's a boy and they can stand up to take care of their business. Hell, he can go in the woods if he needs to.*

The exit ramp led to a small service road with an old run-down building and nothing else. This was clearly not a major metropolitan area, but it didn't matter. Junior would get out, empty his bladder, and we'd be on the road again in a matter of seconds. As the truck came to a screeching halt at the abandoned gas station, Junior jumped out and ran toward what looked like a couple of outhouses. They were shabby buildings on the backside of the gas station, and the closer Junior got to the run-down place, the worse I felt about this stop. I got an eerie feeling in the pit of my stomach and just as I was about to blame it on the coffee I drank at Cracker Barrel, two men pushed up against my door and demanded that I get out. Before I could respond, they were opening the door, grabbing my arm and forcing me to comply. Lisa started to scream from the backseat as the men threw me to the ground. My face smashed into the dirt and gravel mix that made up the service road that led to the gas station from hell.

All I could think about was Junior in that bathroom and what they might do to Lisa who was screaming louder and louder. I knew that as soon as they saw a beautiful teenage girl in the back, what seemed like just a robbery might turn into something more. I had to protect my children, but there was nothing I could do with my face to the ground and this man's knee in my back. They wanted money. What else could they be after? I wouldn't let my mind wander to anything but robbery. They wanted money. I'd give them what I had and they'd let us go. The more I tried to maintain rational thought, the more frightened I became.

"Shut up, dammit," one man yelled at Lisa as he dragged her out of the truck and threw her down beside me.

"Don't hurt her, she's just a child. What do you want?" I managed to blurt out, spitting dirt from my mouth.

"Just keep quiet and you won't get hurt."

All I could think about was Junior coming out of that bathroom and seeing this scene and not knowing what to do. Would he do something stupid? Would they hurt him? One of the men rambled through the truck until he found what he was looking for—my purse. He emptied it onto the ground beside me as his counterpart grabbed my cash and the small gold compact Michael had given me for our tenth anniversary.

"You find anything, man?"

"Yeah, but not much. This worth anything, you think?" he asked his partner while holding up the compact.

"Naw, it's just a stupid make-up thing. Find the money and make that damn girl shut up—all that screaming is making my head hurt."

I tried to remember some of the stuff I'd seen on television. I knew I was supposed to do something in a case like this, but for the life of me I couldn't remember any of that stuff. My face was to the ground, his knee in my back, and I wished I had worn anything but a thin T-shirt. I could feel the rocks digging into my breasts as he pressed his knee down harder and put all his weight on me.

"Is there anything else?" one man asked, directing the question at me.

"No, that's all we have, please don't hurt us. Take what you want, just let us go," I pleaded, knowing Junior would no doubt open that bathroom door any minute.

"She's a pretty little thing, young and sweet," he teased as he rubbed his hand along Lisa's thigh.

I wished I had insisted she not wear that miniskirt. I didn't like the idea of her in something so seductive, but I was trying to be open-minded and hip like the other parents. And now this dirty old fool had his hands on my baby in such a way no man should touch a young girl. Lisa squirmed and started to cry harder.

"Wow, man, look at this."

He had slid Lisa's skirt up enough to reveal most of her behind and the thong underwear. Before I could stop myself, I slid my arm from under his pressure and reached for Lisa. My bare flesh scrubbed against the rocks and gravel. I knew I had broken the skin when I felt the piercing pain all along the underside of my arm. I didn't care. He was not taking this a step further. He would have to kill me first.

"What the hell? Oh, you gonna do something now, huh?" he yelled as he smashed my face back down and yanked my arm back and pinned it under his knee.

I screamed, not only in response to the pain, but to alert Junior. If they were gonna hurt us, screaming wasn't gonna change that. Lisa joined in and we both took it two octaves higher at the top of our lung power. Both men were trying to get us to shut up when the bathroom door started to open. The two men grabbed the valuables from my purse and dashed off.

Junior realized we were lying on the ground and ran to our rescue. With my mind in survival mode, I jumped up off the ground, grabbed Lisa and Junior and shoved them into the truck. My hands were shaking uncontrollably, blood was trickling down my arm, but I managed to grab my purse, scoop up the things from the ground, and jump into the truck. I tried to turn the key in the ignition, but my hands were shaking so badly. I kept looking around into the blackness of the night to make sure the men were gone.

"Shit, why won't this thing . . ."

I couldn't keep my hands still enough to start the truck. Finally Lisa grabbed the key and turned it. The engine started and I slammed the handle into gear and hit the gas. Still looking into the darkness, I tried to keep my thoughts clear enough to remember which way to go.

"Just go, Ma, just drive. We gotta get outta here," Lisa yelled, with tears still flowing.

I got my mind back on the road long enough to get moving in some direction—any direction to get us away from that spot. I remember getting back onto the interstate but I wasn't sure if we were heading north or south. I still couldn't think. So I just drove. We drove for at least fifteen minutes in silence. Lisa was still crying softly. Junior looked at Lisa and back at me, wanting to ask what happened, but knowing he should just keep quiet. After my heart slowed down to an almost normal rate and we were miles from that place, I looked at Junior as if giving him the okay to speak.

"Ma, what happened? Did they hurt you, did they take something?"

"Lisa, are you okay, baby?"

"I'll be fine, Ma. What did they take? Did they hurt you? That man had his knee in your back."

"I'm fine, honey. They got some money, but that's all."

I suddenly felt the pain in my neck from where he had put his weight on me to hold me down. And then I looked at my arm. I tried to hide the blood from the kids, but Junior leaned forward and saw me trying to cover it.

"Do you need to go to the hospital, Ma?"

"No, I'll be okay, we just need to find a place to pull over for the night."

"Are you gonna call the police?"

"And tell them what? I don't even know where we are really. I know we're in Virginia, but I . . . I just need to find some place to stop for the night." The throbbing was getting more intense

With my hands still shaking, Lisa whimpering, and Junior dumb-founded, we kept riding. Turns out we were heading back north, but I didn't care. I pulled off the exit ramp in Petersburg, Virginia, to get a room for the night. With a long sigh, I brought the truck to a stop outside a Holiday Inn Express. By now, Lisa was shaking and Junior had tears in his eyes. He still didn't know what had happened, but he was scared. We sat in the truck for a minute trying to regain our composure. That was a lost cause—it would likely take hours to stop the shaking, so we just got out and tried to act like we hadn't just been robbed.

My hands were still shaking as I handed the desk clerk my credit card. Lisa had her back to us, so I couldn't tell if she was still crying. Junior was right by my side. I got the room key, thanked the clerk, and motioned for the kids to follow me. As much as I was trying to keep my composure, I was scared out of my mind. The harsh reality of the fact that we could have been killed was slowly seeping into my consciousness as I slid the electronic key into the door.

I knew I had to call Michael, but his was the last voice I wanted to hear after something like this. He would be concerned true enough, but he would also blame me for being so shortsighted and pulling off at 1:30 in the morning in the middle of nowhere. Lisa and Junior sat on one of the beds looking at each other, not knowing what to say. I put my keys and purse on the nightstand and picked up the phone to make the dreaded call.

Chapter 7

"Bev, are you okay? You sound terrible."

"Michael, it was terrible. I stopped just so Junior could go to the bathroom and they came out of nowhere."

"Who came out of nowhere, Bev? What happened? Are you guys okay?"

"We're fine now, but two men jumped us at a bathroom stop. I should've waited until I got to a well-lit area like you said, but he had to go and—"

"Bev, what did they do? Did you call the police? Did they hurt you or the kids?"

Michael just kept asking more questions before I could answer the first ones. It was all I could do to keep him from getting in his car and coming to our rescue. He didn't seem upset about my poor judgment. I think he really was just glad we were okay and settling down for the night to get some rest.

"Let me talk to the kids, Bev. I need to hear their voices just so I can sleep tonight," he insisted.

"I'm sure they want to talk to you too, and Michael, we're going to be fine. I just wasn't thinking, that's all. My mind has been all over the place ever since I got that letter from Mabel."

"I didn't mean to sound harsh, Bev. I just can't help but worry about you guys. As it is, I've been a wreck since you left. I should have made the drive with you. I can get Dana to rearrange my schedule and I can meet you all someplace."

I stopped him before he could go on any further. I knew his nerves were getting the best of him. The last place he wanted or needed to be was Vicksburg. He had clients waiting for him to make their problems go away, and my brothers and sisters would only cause him heartache.

"Michael, we'll be fine. Talk to the kids and see for yourself. I appreciate you being so concerned and willing to join us, but it's not necessary. I made a mistake and maybe it was exactly what I needed to keep me on my toes."

By the time they finished talking to Michael, the kids had found one of those music video channels on the TV and were settled in, watching some girl who needed at least another inch added to her skirt to even start being considered decent. They continued bopping their heads to the music and I took a shower to wash away the memory of the evening's events, but no such luck. The more I scrubbed, the more I tasted the dirt from my face being smashed into the ground. Michael suggested I notify someone and file a report or something, but we were in the middle of nowhere and I hadn't bothered to figure out what exit we took. I stood in the shower and cried. I don't know what the tears were about—the frightening robbery, the trip, my miserable marriage—there was so much to cry about and I had been so careful not to let myself feel too much. But this night had been more than I could handle. I backed up against the shower wall and let the tears flow until some of the pain subsided. I couldn't let the kids see me like that. I couldn't let anyone see.

When I got out of the shower, I took an aspirin for the pain in my back and the cuts on my arm. I called the front desk for some Neosporin to put on the cuts. After a few minutes the desk clerk called me back and told me someone was bringing it right up. She asked me what happened. She had noticed the blood on my arm and my soiled T-shirt when we checked in. After I told her we were robbed, she bent over backward to get me anything I needed. I was suddenly grateful for this forty-nine-dollar-a-night haven, Veronica at the front desk, and Leroy who ran over to the 7-Eleven to get the Neosporin cream for me.

I went to bed long before the kids since I had been the one doing the driving. Fortunately, I was able to fall asleep soon after my head hit the pillow. I drifted off to the sounds of rap music and Lisa giving her account to Junior of what had happened. Between his shocked sighs and endless questions, I dozed off into a deep sleep, not even remembering the long journey ahead of me, or, more significantly, why we were making the journey.

Daybreak came too soon. Junior was the first one up, already flipping through channels on the TV set. Lisa slowly rolled over, adjusting her eyes to the light as I opened the blinds on the large picture window. I had been so worked up when we got to the room the night before, I hadn't looked around to take in our surroundings. There were a couple of beds, a bathroom, and a coffeepot for my morning medicine. Besides those things, there wasn't much more—a couple of generic prints on the wall, the standard hotel room carpeting, and a nightstand equipped with telephone, local phone book, and Gideon Bible. I remembered thinking twice about popping open that Bible last night. The robbery had shaken me up so badly, I had almost considered reading it. I hadn't picked up a Bible since . . . well, I couldn't remember the last time. I opened it and flipped through, not knowing what passage to read, until I remembered hearing Mama say that reading the Psalms could heal your heart. My heart and body were in need of some healing, so I read through a portion of Psalm 78:

Give ear, O my people, to my law, incline your ears to the words of my mouth. I will open my mouth in a parable; I will utter dark sayings of old. Which have heard and known, and our fathers have told us. We will not hide them from our children, shewing to the generation to come the praises of the Lord, and His strength, and his wonderful works that He hath done.

I felt better, although I didn't really understand the words I read. Maybe the words would have meant more to me, had I kept the church habit through the years. My parents forced us to go to church when we were little ones and I swore, as soon as I was on my own, I would never set foot in another church. I had held true to that with the exception of my parents' funerals. I guess I put the Bible down back when I dropped the church habit. Nonetheless, those few words, whatever they meant, made me feel better.

"Rise and shine, girl," I chanted, just like my daddy used to do on those mornings when all you needed was just five more minutes.

"Why are we getting up so early?" Lisa mumbled, without looking my way.

"I have about ten hours ahead of me before I can rest my head again. So how about a little concern for the driver?"

"You know, I can help you drive," she added with a sly grin.

"You know what your father told you about interstate driving, young lady. So just get yourself up and get dressed so we can grab a quick bite and get back on the road."

Junior was dressed and sitting down watching those music videos again. I swear it was that same scantily clad young lady from the night before, twirling her behind like those little fast-tail girls at Lisa's school. Lisa's miniskirt wasn't much longer than this girl's. Just as I thought about Lisa's skirt, it popped back into my head— the way that man had touched my baby.

"Lisa, get up, girl, and put something on to cover yourself this time—none of those miniskirts and none of those shorts that got to be cutting off your circulation." While the kids were getting ready and eating the complimentary breakfast, I tried to find something to do so my mind wouldn't drift back to the night before. I grabbed a local newspaper, looking for some inspiration for this knockout book I was gonna write when I got back to Melrose.

When I travel, I love to get a local paper and see what's important enough to make the news. The national news is always the same from paper to paper, but the local stuff could be a trip sometimes. Some of the things that were called news never ceased to amaze me. This paper had several stories about hot political races in the area. Mudslinging and self-boasting were all over the five or so pages that made up the Wednesday edition. There it was on the back page, almost hidden by an add for some type of sex enhancement drug. A story about a grandfather who left his two-year-old granddaughter in a hot car all day.

The absentminded granddad left the baby in the car for eight hours while he went to work and then ran an errand. He was supposed to drop the baby off at day care, but instead forgot she was in the car and went on to work as usual. Temperatures were lingering in the mid to low nineties, so after a few hours the baby died of heat exhaustion. The grandfather was taken into custody, but hadn't been charged yet. What would they charge him with? I wondered. Maybe involuntary manslaughter. What was going through the grandfather's mind as he sat in jail waiting to find out what was going to happen to him for killing his own granddaughter? What were the baby's parents saying? Amazing story, and there it was, on the back page of the paper. The sex enhancement ad had larger print. *What a shame*. Then Lisa and Junior finally gave the signal that they were ready to hit the road.

With a decent-sized drink in hand, each of us jumped into the truck confident that we would have a much better day of traveling ahead of us. After an hour of good radio stations fading in and out, Junior started with the questions.

"Ma, why are we going to Mississippi anyway?"

That was the question I did not want to answer. I knew I couldn't give him a simple answer, such as, "to settle some land issue." Junior was a young man after details and since there wasn't anything on the radio and Lisa was in her own world with her CD player, and not about to share it, Junior had no reason to keep the questions to a minimum.

"Your aunts and uncles and I need to decide what to do with the land your grandfather left us when he died."

"I didn't know granddaddy had any land," Lisa chimed in, letting us know she wasn't really so into that CD player, and instead she had just been ignoring us.

"Yeah, he had fifteen acres of land almost right on the river. The house we grew up in was on the land, but now it's just land and the economic development people want to do something with it, other than just let it sit there."

"Why didn't you all do something with it?"

That was certainly the million-dollar question, but I wasn't about to get into that with them.

"Well, none of us really owned the land outright after Daddy died. He kind of didn't really specify who would decide what to do with it . . . so no one wanted to do anything that the others might not agree with."

"So, you're gonna sell the land for money," Junior added.

"No, fool, they gonna sell it for poker chips," Lisa teased.

Junior looked like he didn't know what to make of her comment.

"With all the casinos springing up in Vicksburg, poker chips might not be a bad idea, Lisa," I laughed.

Junior sat silently only for a few minutes to let the poker theme fade out, and then the questions started again.

"So, what exactly is gonna happen to the land?"

"I don't exactly know. I think they need to use it to extend a road because of all the businesses and things that are springing up in that area now."

"What happened to the house?"

I knew the questions would go on until we crossed the Mississippi state line if I didn't just go ahead and tell him the story. I don't know why I'd never told him the story before. I guess by the time

Junior was old enough, I had written those fools in Mississippi off, and what happened to them and that land was not my concern.

"You see, Junior, this is how it happened. Like I told you before, your grandfather, Johnston Tayloe, worked at the National Military Park. We'll take a tour of the park if we finish with our business in time. The park was created a long time ago, way back in 1899, to mark one of the most important battles of the Civil War. I know you read about the Civil War in school, so now you know that Mommy's hometown was a major player in the South defending itself against the North. The city of Vicksburg was important because it's located high in the bluffs, so it was a pretty good fortress to guard the Mississippi. I know you know something about fortresses as much as you and those bad-ass friends of yours used to tear up my backyard building them."

Both kids were as attentive as I had seen them in a long time.

"Anyway, Vicksburg was known as the 'Gibraltar of the Confederacy.' The city surrendered on July 4, 1863, and that gave the North control of the river. If we get a chance to visit the park while we're in Vicksburg, you'll see monuments and markers, and miles and miles of reconstructed trenches and earthworks. You'll almost wish you were ten again and had some of your buddies with you to play in those trenches. There's a restored gunboat and of course the National Cemetery, which is the part of the park where your grandfather worked."

"Ma, how do you know so much about all that stuff? You sound worst than my history teacher," Junior joked.

"You can't spend all your life in Vicksburg and not know the significance of the place. I didn't just learn that stuff in school. Your grandfather gave us his own version, which included some stuff you don't get in your history books. And he knew what he was talking about, too, cause he worked at the military cemetery."

"What did he do at the cemetery? That sure isn't a job I would want. Too many dead people," Lisa added her two cents' worth.

"It ain't the dead ones, but the lives ones you got to worry about.

That's what your grandfather would always say when we joked with him about working at the cemetery."

"So what did he do there?" Junior insisted.

"Well," I continued my history lesson with two eager listeners, "the cemetery is a hundred and sixteen acres and there are more than seventeen hundred soldiers buried there. That's more than any other national cemetery. Some of the folks buried there are either wives or children of veterans and government workers. When we get there you'll see upright headstones—those are for known veterans. The small square blocks with just a number on them are for unknown soldiers. Daddy said there was no one famous buried there, but then again, anyone who dies serving his country is famous."

"Ma, you still haven't said what Granddaddy did at the cemetery," Junior reminded me.

"Oh, yeah, well, it's simple enough, really. I told you the cemetery itself is a hundred and sixteen acres with all those headstones and markers. Somebody has to keep the place up. Because it's a military cemetery, it has to be kept up to the military code for cemeteries. Your grandfather was in charge of making sure the grounds were kept up according to code. He had a crew of men that worked for him, doing the simple stuff like cutting the grass, which could only be a certain height. They tended the trees to make sure dead limbs that had fallen to the ground didn't just lie around for days. They also made sure visitors and tourists didn't mess the place up. You know tourists—they can even trash a cemetery. Grandfather's crew did a bunch of other stuff, but the main thing was keeping the cemetery looking like something Vicksburg and the whole country could be proud of."

Lisa and Junior both were hanging on my every word. I was shocked by how little they knew about my hometown. But then again, who would they have learned it from but me? I continued.

"I remember times when your grandfather had to leave the house in the middle of the night after a big storm to make sure there wasn't any damage to the cemetery. Sometimes it would take until daybreak to pick up downed limbs and get the place looking in tip-top shape in time for tourists or visiting family members. At the end of each day, someone on Daddy's crew had to comb the entire place to make sure there wasn't stuff left on the grave sites. You'd expect to see flowers or a special gift left expressing sentiment, but they would also find the occasional McDonald's coffee cup on one of the gravestones. I'm not sure what the sentiment in that was."

The kids laughed and talked about how they couldn't wait to see the place and how we just had to make time to go. I drove on feeling pretty good about sharing my family history with my kids. So much bad had happened in the last few years since I'd visited Mississippi, I could hardly remember the good stuff about the place. I couldn't help but smile as they joked about lazy tourists peeing in the cemetery and teenagers sneaking away from their parents to make out. By the time they finished their made-up accounts of life at the National Cemetery, it was time to stop for lunch. My mention of a McDonald's coffee cup sparked an interest in a certain curly redheaded clown named Ronald. We searched for the golden arches and pulled off the exit ramp.

While the kids were getting their food and checking out the local scenery, I tried to reach Michael. After six rings the answering service kicked in and this time I just didn't feel like being treated as if I was no better than one of his clients. In fact, I was sure his clients could get to him quicker than I could. I punched the END button before the voice on the other end could finish his pleasant spill—the recording I'd heard one time too many.

It had crossed my mind a time or two that Michael might have been doing something he had no business doing during those late nights. Perhaps he was stepping out on me and dillydallying with one of those short-skirt-wearing secretaries at the office. Or was he seeing one of his former clients, some lost soul he'd saved from bankruptcy and she just had to show him how grateful she was? But in the end, I knew Michael was just being Michael. Incapable of too much physical affection and lost in the work ethic that drove his entire family. They were all like that. It's like someone had whispered in their ear that they would be sent back to Haiti if they didn't work at least eighty hours a week. Michael acted like the boat would be waiting for him at the first sign of letting up or enjoying life.

The kids and I spent most of our family vacations without him. He would occasionally join us for a day or two, but he never spent an entire week away from work. I made my peace with just spending time with the kids. Whenever the loneliness got too unbearable, I just went shopping. Since I made my own money, and plenty of it, I shopped a lot.

I turned the cell phone off. I didn't want him to be able to contact me either. I needed this break. Although I would have preferred the south of France instead of Mississippi, in either case Michael was the last person I wanted to hear from.

The kids got back into the truck and I started with my most stirring rendition of "On the Road Again." They both laughed and covered their ears, shouting all kinds of craziness to get me to stop singing. I didn't know what I would do without my kids. They certainly made the days bearable. It was the nights I had to work on— no kids, no shopping. Something had to change.

Chapter 8

With a Big Mac tugging on my eyelids, I made my way down the interstate. After no more than a few minutes the kids were asleep and I was alone with my thoughts. I didn't even bother to fiddle with the radio because music was the last thing on my mind. As much as I was dreading this trip, there was also a hint of anticipation, good anticipation. I hadn't been to Vicksburg in years and things were bound to have changed.

I knew of a few changes from conversations with Mabel. She mentioned the gambling boats on the river. She talked about the great things Cedar Inn had done to make that "fancied-up place," as she called it, even more fancy. We were also set to arrive just in time to catch *Gold in the Hills*, a melodrama at the Parkside Playhouse. Although Mabel wasn't into stuff like that, she did mention that it would be a good place to take the kids. So my weekend was all set. I would meet with those fools Thursday night, then meet with the economic development people and the bank Friday. Saturday would be filled with more Vicksburg history than two teenagers could stand. We'd spend the morning touring the national park and cemetery where Daddy worked, grab lunch at one of the great new restaurants downtown overlooking the river, and then we'd be off to *Gold in the Hills.*

The drama is actually the world's longest running, listed in the *Guinness Book of World Records.* The kids would surely get a kick out of the singing and cancan dancers. Scheduling these outings was my way of making sure to not spend too much time with my siblings after we made our decision concerning the land. No doubt I would upset someone and they would do their best to ruin my trip—unless they couldn't find me. And that was my plan: get lost in Vicksburg enjoying my hometown with my children and avoiding the awkward relationship with my brothers and sisters.

I'm usually not one to avoid confrontation and awkward situations, but you have to know when to throw in the towel. I have spent too much of my life trying to appease ignorance and keep peace in my own house. My goal now is to just do something with that land, so we won't continue to be the laughing stock of the black community in Vicksburg. Everyone knew the Tayloe family was at odds over that land. That became common knowledge when the house got flooded six years ago and we just bulldozed it after letting it sit there until they condemned it.

Mabel let me know how much people in the community were talking about the Tayloe family. She told me in one of her monthly conversations that that old crazy-ass Bigun Spinks had something to say about the land.

"*Sis, you won't believe who had the nerve to stop me in de grocery store and ask 'bout the lan.*"

"*No, Mabel, I have no idea.*"

"*Bigun Spinks walked right up to me and asked me what we was gonna do with the lan. I tol him I didn't know and besides, it weren't none of his business. He kept looking at me like I stunk or somethin', then said we was all a bunch of fools if we let that lan go back to the white man. He said we should be shamed of ourselves to watch Daddy work all dat hard, and then act stupid 'bout that lan and let dem white folk come right in and take it from us.*"

70

"Well, Mabel, I wouldn't worry about it, honey. You are talking about Bigun, he's not the smartest man in town and who cares what he has to say anyway."

I didn't let Mabel in on it, but I was troubled by what Bigun had said. I knew Bigun wasn't intelligent enough to come to that conclusion on his own, so he must be talking behind someone. It hurt my feelings a little to know people were talking about my daddy. I knew how much Daddy prided himself in doing right, so folk wouldn't talk about us. But they were talking, and they were right, and this trip would put all the ugliness to an end.

Daddy bought that land during a time when it was a miracle for a black man to even try to accomplish such a feat. Most of the white folk were amazed that Johnston Tayloe even had the money, let alone the knowledge to take on purchasing land and having a home built on it. The one big thing Daddy missed in all the proceedings was the insurance. Since the land was in the floodplain, he should have been required to purchase flood insurance, but no one ever mentioned it. There was so much to making the purchase, clearing the land and then starting on the house, that Daddy didn't even think about the Mississippi rolling over her banks and nipping at the edge of our land. He certainly didn't consider that a year after his death, the river would spill over its bed and swallow up so much land that water stood three feet deep inside the house. After the floodwaters receded, many of the houses in that area were condemned. The federal buyout program kicked in and most of the landowners moved to higher ground. Since there was no one living in the family house, it was easy to just let it sit there for a while.

After a few months, all eyes were on the Tayloe house, since it was the only one in the area still standing with the same red paint marks warning nosey onlookers to keep off the premises. Another month went by and the house was condemned. I was still shaken up from the way things had gone at Daddy's funeral that I wanted to do anything but set my foot inside the state of Mississippi. So, Grace and Andrew made the call and had the house bulldozed and the debris cleared from the land. I sent them my check to cover my portion of the cost, which was actually my portion plus Mabel's since she was between jobs at the time. Mabel is the only person I know who can spend years between jobs. But I digress. Anyway, the land was cleared and everyone in the area waited to see what we would do next. And they were still waiting.

The area hadn't flooded in recent years and from what Mabel told me, there were "barriers" of some kind put up so they could develop the area without worrying about flooding destroying progress. The only thing undeveloped was the Tayloe land. But that would all change after this week.

I was deep in thought, planning what I would say to any stupid remarks of keeping the land, when Lisa and Junior both woke up talking about wanting something to eat. If I didn't know better, I'd have sworn those two had a tapeworm sometimes. Instead of driving on, we decided to stop for the night, and then get dinner and a hotel room. This trip was wearing on me. I never remembered the drive being such a taxing one. But in times past I had never been robbed, nor had I been tied up in knots about confronting my family.

We had dinner at a nice restaurant and bedded down at another Holiday Inn Express. The kids were getting tired of being trapped in that truck and spending their nights in cramped-up hotel rooms. They would be okay as soon as they laid eyes on the Cedar Grove Inn. I called Michael.

"Hi, Bev. How are things going so far? Has the traffic been heavy?" Michael asked sleepily.

"It's been okay. The kids are loving every minute of it," I said, giggling as Lisa gave me a stern look and a snarl.

"You guys be sure to rest up good before getting back on the road in the morning. Vicksburg will be there whenever you arrive, so don't try to break any records."

"You know me, baby," I replied in my sexiest voice.

"Yeah, I know you, that's why I mentioned it. Seriously, Bev, I worry about you guys. I know you can handle yourself, but you all are still my responsibility and, above all, you and those hardheaded younguns are my life."

Michael sounded like a man missing his home-cooked meals and loudmouth children a little too much. I assured him we would be fine and said good night. He kept stalling, trying to keep me on the phone as if the hundreds of miles would disappear through those phone lines.

As I hung up the phone I imagined the feeling of missing my husband. The feeling of wanting him next to me in the bed. Feeling his body warm against my own. Michael is handsome in his own quirky, smart-guy kind of way. He's 5'10" and no more than 180 pounds of muscle. Despite his rigorous work schedule, he finds time to work out, so he has a nice tight body. His light brown skin is as clear as a baby's behind. He takes good care of himself and his clothes are the finest tailored suits at Nordstrom's. His causal clothes are usually the latest by Ralph Lauren. He sports a hand-crafted timepiece we picked up at Tiffany & Co. during one of our last trips to New York. Handsome man, with his head in the right place, but his body never close enough to mine. I could see him in my mind's eye and I could smell his Gucci cologne as if he were lying right beside me, but he wasn't. My daydream ended with the frightening reality that it had never been that way. It had always been something I desired, but never got. Michael liked the security the family gave him, knowing we were there and all. He was lonely for the thought of having us around, not lonely for us.

Lisa and Junior were already in bed, so I slipped into bed beside Lisa and let fatigue take over the crazy thoughts of cuddling with a sexy man who wanted me as much as he wanted his next breath. I imagined a tall, dark, sexy chocolate man with arms that would wrap me up and protect me from all the craziness life was throwing my way. As I drifted in and out of awareness, I imagined.

* * *

Check-in at the Cedar Inn starts at 3:00 and if my calculations were right we would be pulling up to the inn just after 3:30. Lisa and Junior were buzzing with anticipation, not really knowing what to expect when we finally got there. Lisa had a relationship with Mabel's son Trey, but I don't think they'd talked in the last couple of years. I could tell she was excited about getting to see her "ole homey," as she called him. Junior was just excited in general. It was all new to him. He was only six the last time we were in Vicksburg, so he was walking into the situation with a clean slate. Lucky kid.

During the next few hours we continued our lesson of Vicksburg and the Tayloe family. Junior started with the questions as soon as we were on the road. But this time he didn't want to know about the history or the cemetery—he wanted to know about his grandparents, aunts, and uncles. This was a conversation I definitely wasn't ready for.

"So, Ma, Aunt Grace is the oldest—she's the tall one, right?"

"Yeah, Grace is the tall one."

I went on telling Junior all the basics about his Aunt Grace: she was tall, didn't have a husband or children—all standard stuff—but as I talked, I couldn't help but remember a time when Grace wasn't such a bad person to be around.

After college, Grace started the job she still works today, as administrative assistant at the national park. Most people thought she held on to that job because it was a no-brainer and gave her plenty of time to stay in everybody's business, but I thought differently. Once upon a time Grace had a man in her life. Leroy Anderson was his name and, if memory serves me right, he was rather nice-looking. Leroy was intelligent and was the accountant who handled the books for the Military Park. Leroy and Grace met right there at the park and started a hot and heavy relationship that kept them both on a tight leash. The two of them were just about to start living together when Leroy started getting the headaches. He took a few days off work and then days turned into weeks. I don't know why he waited so long to get it checked out, but by the time he went to the doctor, it was too late. He had a brain tumor and even with surgery his chances were slim. Grace was right by his side through the operation, and the days and nights that Leroy didn't even know he was alive. After the surgery, Leroy's mental capacity was the equivalent of a three-year-old child's. He could talk, but not plain enough for most people to understand. Grace bought the house she lives in now and moved Leroy in with her. She took care of him day and night, until the morning Leroy didn't wake up.

I always thought Grace kept the job at the park because it was her way of hanging on to the memory of a vibrant, successful Leroy. Her office was right next to his and even though accountants have come and gone, I think she still wants to keep her spot next to Leroy. Grace didn't sell the house either, like everyone suggested. She turned Leroy's room into a guest room. The room is furnished with all the things they picked out for their house together. I also believe Grace never really dated again because she had found her one true love. Perhaps she couldn't find anyone who ever measured up, but that was a Grace Junior would never know. That was a Grace I had all but forgotten.

At 3:34 PM eastern standard time, we pulled into the front parking area of the Cedar Grove Inn. Others were arriving at the same time with that same wide-eyed look I had during my first stay at Cedar Grove. Junior was opening the truck door before I even came to a complete stop. Lisa was trying to keep her cool, but she too was ready to see the place I had been ranting and raving about since I announced they were making this trip with me.

Check-in was at the main house, an intimidating two-story structure with four huge pillars anchoring the first- and second-story porches. The hostess met us at the front desk in the huge foyer. Everything was immaculate and the period furniture took me back to the Old South. I giggled under my breath, knowing that in the Old South, I wouldn't likely be anything more than a "house nigger" at this fine establishment. But today, my kids and I were customers, my money as green as the next man's, ready to be treated with the Southern hospitality that makes Vicksburg live up to the name "Red Carpet City of the South."

The inn was much nicer than I remembered from past visits, and before checking into our room we took the tour of the main house. Lisa and Junior followed Lydia, our tour guide, through the front foyer into the double parlor. There were several beautiful fireplaces spaced throughout the area, and if it weren't ninety degrees outside, sitting next to a cozy fire might be appealing. The drapery, wall hangings and furniture were all period pieces. We left the double parlor and went into the formal dining room. The table was set and ready for eight very special quests. The decor of this room let you know for sure that if you're eating in here, you're somebody. Across the hall from the dining room was the ballroom. Lydia let us know that this space could be rented out for special occasions, for a reasonable fee. I snickered under my breath at the thought of their definition of a reasonable fee. Toward the back of the house were the bar and a restaurant called Andre's. Both the bar and restaurant were empty, but Lydia assured us that by happy hour, both would be humming with activity.

When I made the reservations, I booked the Centennial Suite, a large, beautifully furnished gallery suite with a king-size bed, a second bedroom, spacious parlor, two fireplaces, a wet bar, refrigerator and microwave, spa tub, double vanity, and separate shower. As I breathlessly walked around the living area, Junior made his way to the balcony that overlooked the grounds, and there it was—the most splendid view of the Mississippi. We all stood there speechless, taking in the view, the sounds of peace and tranquility, and the smell of something sweet baking in the restaurant in the rear of the main house.

Junior snapped out of his daze first and announced that he was going back out to the truck to get our bags. Lisa and I both flopped down on a wicker sofa on the balcony and continued our gaze out over the river. Engulfed by so much elegance and romance, I suddenly felt like Scarlett O'Hara in *Gone with the Wind.*

"Lisa, Lisa, girl, where is your mind?"

"Ma, this is phat," she murmured, with her eyes closed.

Phat wasn't exactly the term I had in mind, but it communicated her feeling perfectly. I left her to her phatness and made my way to the mansion bar for a mint julep. I'm not usually a mint julep fan, but it just seemed appropriate surrounded by all that antebellum stuff. As I sipped the julep, soft piano music started in the background. I needed to give Grace a call to let her know we were in town, but as the music continued, the julep started to take effect and all I could think was, "Frankly, Grace, I don't give a damn."

After downing a couple of juleps, I ventured out onto the grounds. The layout was breathtaking. The inn is surrounded by five acres of gardens and I was determined to see every inch of the place. There were several gardens near our room, but there was only one with another black person strolling through it. I assumed he was a groundskeeper, since, according to Grace, intelligent colored folk didn't waste their money at a place like this. I watched him inspect the flowers and then the soil. He went to the next plant and stooped down to take in the fragrance.

"Excuse me—I didn't see you there," he said, as if apologizing for blocking the walkway.

"You're okay. I was just taking a walk. Do you work here?"

"No, no, I'm a guest. I'm in town on business and, well, we got things wrapped up early so I decided to stay on a few extra days and enjoy the place. What about you?"

I felt silly for automatically assuming he was hired help.

"I'm here on family business, I guess you can say."

I was stumbling over my words and I knew it had something to do with this handsome specimen sniffing flowers in front of me.

"You're from here?" he asked.

"No, well, yes, I grew up here, but I live in Massachusetts now."

"This is a far cry from Massachusetts," he said, laughing and continuing to inspect the flowers.

"Yes, it is," I added, hoping to end this conversation before the juleps made me say something I would live to regret. I looked up at the bright sunny sky just as the sun made its way behind a cloud. I felt a tingle in my stomach that I hadn't felt in years. I blamed it on the alcohol, but I'd had plenty of alcohol in the last seventeen years without tingles. Mr. Flower Sniffer was stirring up a side of Beverly I was sure had died after Junior was born.

I looked down at my cell phone. I turned it back on even though I knew it wouldn't ring. He wouldn't call. It was only 4:00 in the afternoon. He'd never just call this early in the day. We had been robbed the night before and still he wouldn't call. The children and I were just his trophies, his accomplishments. He stuck his chest out and spoke about us proudly at company gatherings, but he didn't know us. He certainly didn't know me. He didn't know what I had been feeling, or not feeling. He didn't know I hadn't been tingling, and, more importantly, he didn't care. I wished he'd call and save me from myself. Didn't he know I'd want more?

"Are you here alone?"

The Flower Sniffer startled me back to reality and this time he was standing right in front of me, too close for comfort. I'd stumbled over my words before, but this time I was sure a silly schoolgirl giggle would tumble out. The tingling started again.

"No, my kids are inside. They aren't accustomed to this Southern heat."

"And your husband?"

"No, just the kids and myself. Just us," I babbled.

"Maybe we could get a drink later. I hear they have an excellent Long Island Iced Tea. After a stroll in the garden, a drink would hit the spot."

I got the impression we weren't really talking about Long Island Iced Tea. He was flirting and he was getting as good as he was giving.

"Yes, I bet that would hit the spot." I smiled and licked my lips, knowing full well I should have taken my married behind back inside.

"I'm in the Colonial Suite. Victor Mabrey. And your name?" he offered, extending his hand.

"I'm, I'm Beverly Dunn," I stammered as I shook his hand—soft tender hands, not the hands of a man who did hard labor. They weren't manicured or fussed over, but big, strong, yet tender to the touch.

"Beverly Bradford Dunn, the author?"

And he reads too.

"One and the same."

"Well, get out. I read your stuff all the time. I love mysteries and I travel a lot, so I have plenty of time to read. I just finished your latest, *Swear By Your Honor*."

"Yep, that's me."

"But you're black. I would have thought . . ."

"Yes, last time I checked. Black woman, two kids, lives in Massachusetts."

"Married?"

I wasn't sure what my answer would be. Since I'm really not Beverly Bradford Dunn, I really don't have to be married. I wanted the little game to continue and, more importantly, I wanted to see where the tingle would lead.

"Yes, married." I chickened out.

"Well, I just can't believe this. Beverly Bradford Dunn in Vicksburg, Mississippi, strolling through the same garden."

I couldn't believe it either. I wanted to ask where he had been strolling seventeen years ago, but I knew this conversation had to end before I lost my home training and joined him for some of that good ole iced tea . . . and more of that good feeling I had been longing for.

Chapter 9

Victor Mabrey left the garden before I did. He seemed to sense my uneasiness with the flirting, so he made up some excuse about making calls and left me alone. I was by myself in that garden, but far from alone. I blamed the thoughts on the alcohol in the juleps, but most of it was just a woman in need of a friend, companion, and a lover.

I plucked a flower from one of the bushes in the garden and let the fragrance and softness of the petals tease my senses. Tease my senses the same way Victor had teased my emotions. Attractive black men were not the norm in Melrose, Massachusetts. I felt like I was losing all my home training. I knew better than to flirt with a strange man in the middle of a garden. I hadn't noticed a ring on his finger, and I had removed mine the night after we were robbed. I didn't want to take any chances, so I locked the ring in the glove box of the truck.

So, to Victor Mabrey, I was a woman without a wedding ring, two kids, a missing husband . . . and a thirst for a good Long Island. I blushed just thinking about the implications. I felt kind of sexy and attractive for the first time in I don't know when. I hadn't felt sexy when I met Michael. Most of what we shared were intellectual moments. When he found out I was a writer, he probed my mind with deep philosophical questions based on things he had studied in law school. I liked that. It challenged that part of me. I thought about things in a whole new way after talking to Michael. At twenty years old I was impressed by his knowledge and desire for more, more from life and more from a relationship. With Michael it wasn't about physical prowess and natural urges. His mind intrigued me, but after lonely nights in a cold, damp Cambridge apartment, his intellect wasn't enough.

I had never been the attractive one of the girls in my family. Grace was the knockout. Mabel was slow-minded, but still pretty. That's how that bum that she calls Trey's daddy knocked her up. Boys wanted Mabel even though they knew she couldn't carry a decent conversation with them. But me, I was the bookworm. Not much to look at and too intimidated to do anything about it. I made my peace to just be comfortable. I wore comfortable jeans and sweaters when it was cold out and jeans and T-shirts during the summer. Nothing else. Tennis shoes and old beat-up sandals covered my feet in appropriate weather, and my hair . . . well, that was another story. Most of the time I didn't bother with curlers or fussy stuff like that. I just pulled it back in a ponytail or tied it up in a bun. As long as it was clean, that was enough. Plain Jane.

But sitting in the garden at thirty-seven years old with my hair tied up too tight, my jeans fitting too loose and a T-shirt that had seen better days, I felt sexy. I felt seductive, and the sensation wouldn't go away. I looked down at the sandals on my feet, and that's when I saw the business card.

Victor Mabrey had dropped his card. More than likely on purpose, but I didn't want to read too much into it. I couldn't hold the smile in any longer. I stuck the card in my jeans pocket, leaned back on the garden bench, and smiled from ear to ear. The game was far from over. He had put the ball in my court.

I went back to my suite to nap and let the buzz subside before calling Grace. Lisa and Junior were out exploring the grounds. The phone rang.

"Michael," I whispered, before picking up the receiver, then "Yes, dear, I see you found me."

"Yes, I did, but I'm not sure I'm the dear you were expecting."

It was Victor. I didn't have time to think. He was laughing on the other end. I felt flushed with embarrassment and excitement at the same time.

"I'm sorry, I was expecting my husband. I—how did you get my number?"

"The numbers are posted in the inn lobby. You left your credit card at the bar earlier. I found it and started to turn it in, but decided to just get it to you myself. I hope that's okay."

"Sure. I can't believe I was so careless."

"I'll bring it right up, if that's okay. You're in the Centennial, right?"

"Yes," I answered. He hung up the phone.

It wasn't okay for him to come up. The kids were out and I was acting too giddy. I rushed to the bathroom to look myself over. Everything looked just like it always did. My hair was unkempt, just like it was when he started flirting with me in the garden. I was wearing the same white Nike T-shirt and Guess jeans. This pair fit me kind of loose, but I turned around to get a quick butt shot anyway. Why do women do that? Gotta see what the booty looks like to the opposite sex. Mine was a normal-looking butt, filling out the jeans, but not tight enough to get the whole picture of what was inside. I giggled just thinking about the fact that I was not quite filling out a pair of size-ten jeans. For most of my life a size ten would have cut off my circulation. But for the last seven years it had all been different. I don't know if it was my father's death, breaking off my relationship with my siblings, or my lackluster marriage, but something prompted me to call that personal trainer.

It was the most frightening thing I had done in a long time, and I wasn't sure why. I found the number on a poster at the supermarket. Flex Appeal was the name of the business and the picture of a shapely man and woman on the poster made the name's true meaning crystal clear. The no-waisted, big-breasted, tan woman and her equally hunky partner were flexing true enough, but it was raw sex appeal that they were selling.

I didn't want anyone to see me checking out the poster, so I acted like I was reading the one next to it about a gospel concert at the local Methodist church. I was looking directly at the church poster, but couldn't tell you half of what it said. I slanted my head to the side, just enough to read the numbers. "555-2849," I whispered once, just to log it in my memory bank. I shook my head like I had finished reading about the church concert and made my way out the door still saying, "555-2849."

I called from my cell phone and when Brian Kane answered, I almost hung up.

"Yes, I'd like to get some information about your personal training program."

"Sure. I could go over the basics with you over the phone, but if you could make an appointment to stop by our place, I could answer all your questions and show you some top-of-the-line fitness training. If you have time, we could even do a practice run, just to see where you are."

Brian was acting as if he had already made the sale. He kept pitching the great service and benefits he had to offer. I listened, still thinking I would have been better off going to the gospel concert than to a gym.

After one meeting with Brian, I was hooked. I started an eight-week program that turned into two years. Forty pounds and three clothes sizes later, the new Beverly hit the scene. I couldn't wait to show off my tight little ass and pouting breasts, but who did I plan to show them to? Michael was genuinely impressed with my results, but since he's always been borderline anorexic, it didn't impact him the way I'd hoped it would. After two years and thousands of dollars, I had the body I thought was supposed to get the man. I had the man, so I made myself content that I was healthier and would likely live longer for committing to take better care of my body and keep the weight off.

Now, finally, someone was noticing the body I'd paid all that money for. I hadn't caught Victor looking at my body, but they always do. He commented about my nice smile, which in "men's language" actually means "nice breasts."

I paced around the suite nervously, trying to figure out what to do with this man in my private quarters. I walked back into the bathroom and looked into the mirror again. This time, I pulled the band off my ponytail and let my hair fall free. The newly permed coal-black locks fell just below my shoulders and I smiled, just like the smile I saw on Lisa's face when she packed her hip-huggers.

"Whew, somebody needs to whip my behind," I said, giggling.

The knock sent a chill up my spine and I hated myself for feeling what I was feeling. I walked to the door slowly, as if delaying things would ease my nervousness. When I opened the door, he was standing there with the same smile he'd flashed my way in the garden when he made the drink offer.

"Come on in. I can't believe I left my credit card down there. Must've had one too many. I'm never that careless. It's a good thing you found it. There's no telling what could have happened if that card got into the wrong hands."

I couldn't for the life of me figure out why I was talking so much. I couldn't shut up. My mouth simply wouldn't stop moving . . . until he grabbed my hand.

"It's okay. We all forget sometimes. It's no big deal. I found it, and now you have it back."

It wasn't the lost credit card that had me acting so silly. It was being alone with him and the prospect that his offering to bring me the card was more than just a kind act from a concerned stranger.

"Yeah, you're right. I have it back, so why worry."

He let go of my hand and started looking around the suite.

"Nice place. You went all out for this one."

"Yeah, I've always liked this inn, and, well, I figured I might as well get a nice room for myself and ummm . . . the kids."

I mentioned the kids on purpose to remind myself that they might walk in any minute and wonder why this strange man was in our room.

"How old are they? The kids?"

"Ummm, my son is fourteen and Lisa, well, she's sixteen and going to be a senior in high school."

"Wow, I would have never imagined you had kids that old. You've taken care of yourself—that or you had babies when you were twelve," he said, laughing.

He was so comfortable and talking to me as if we were old friends. He had to know having him in my room freaked me out. I was also flattered by his compliment. I tried to relax or at least give the appearance of relaxing.

"So you use a pen name?"

"Yes, how did you—oh, that's right, the credit card gave me away."

"Yeah, I put two and two together and figured you were Beverly, just with a different last name."

He was too comfortable for my taste. I couldn't stop fidgeting, so I sat down on the couch, hoping the change in position would help. I had tried so hard not to stare at him too much in the garden, but now, with him standing right in front of me, too close for comfort, I couldn't look away. At 5'11", maybe 190 pounds, he was wearing a wrinkled pair of khaki Dockers, held up by a black leather belt. His shirt was just as wrinkled, but with the arms cut out, his shirt was not what was getting my attention. He was sporting a pair of baby dreads, which would normally be a turnoff to me, but they worked with the rest of his look. In his left ear, a diamond stud twinkled as the overhead light hit it. I tried to find something to do with my hands, but all I could do was fumble the credit card from hand to hand.

"Am I making you nervous?"

"No, not at all," I lied.

"I travel a lot and I'm just accustomed to making myself at home with new faces everywhere I go. I didn't mean to just barge in. And, my shameless flirting out in the garden—forgive me. I just don't run across beautiful black women in my line of work."

Beautiful—now, that's a word I've never heard in a description of Beverly Lamark. And he was admitting to flirting with me.

"That's okay. Harmless flirting never hurt anyone."

"I'm not sure your husband would agree with that line of thinking. Well, I've bothered you enough. I'm gonna head out and see what else Vicksburg has to offer. I'll see you around," he said, reaching for the door.

I didn't want him to leave, but I knew he was doing the right thing. When I looked down at his feet, he was wearing a pair of brown sandals. They worked perfectly with the rest of his outfit.

"Yeah, we'll be in town for a few days, so maybe I will see you around."

He had opened the door and was on his way out, but suddenly stopped and turned back around as if he had forgotten something. He shut the door and walked back into the suite and took a seat on the couch.

"Listen, Beverly, can I be completely honest with you?"

I wasn't sure how to answer. So I didn't.

"I am intrigued by the fact that you are the person responsible for all those great books I've enjoyed over the years. I've read all your stuff, so when I found out who you were, I kinda felt like I knew you already. But then I started to get the impression that you are nothing like the person I imagined writing those books. And now, I'm even more intrigued. I'd really love to get to know the real Beverly."

He paused. I looked at his face and into his eyes for the first time—nice brown eyes with a thin mustache above his top lip and a well-trimmed goatee beneath his bottom lip. I watched his mouth as he carefully formed the words.

"I know it sounds crazy, but I just wanted to be honest. I didn't want you to think I was some weirdo. Something about you got my attention, and I can't seem to shake it. I cleverly dropped my card in the garden, hoping you'd find it. And then when I found your credit card at the bar, I took advantage of the opportunity. I know you're in town for family business and you've got your kids and your life, but . . . well, maybe if this had been another time, another place."

He got up and walked toward the door with his head bent down in embarrassment. I still hadn't spoken. There was so much I wanted to say, but no words would form. I wanted to tell him that I knew exactly what he was talking about. He had my attention as well, but it was just too wrong. He closed the door behind him and I heard his footsteps getting fainter and fainter in the distance.

I was still holding the credit card. I wanted his words to stop ringing in my ear. *Why him, why now? Another time, another place is exactly right. But not this time, not this place.* I lifted the credit card to my nose. It still had the scent of his cologne on it. I sniffed hard and closed my eyes, wishing it were another time, another place.

I tossed the credit card down on the coffee table and ran to the bathroom to get myself together. Splashing cold water on my face, I tried not to look at myself in the mirror, but there I was. I realized for the first time I was looking into the eyes of a woman I had never seen. A risk-taking, free-spirited Beverly was staring back at me and she scared the hell out of me. I had always been responsible, sensible, and loyal—especially loyal.

I ran out of the bathroom and rushed to call Grace. She sounded busy, so I let her know we were in town and getting settled at the inn. When I hung up the phone, I was still too confused to know what to do. His presence was still in the room, still pulling at me, so I grabbed my keys and headed out the door.

Chapter 10

I found Junior and Lisa in one of the gardens near the back of the property.

"Hey guys, I'm going to run out for a minute, but you can hang out here. Just don't get into any trouble. Go back up to the room and get cleaned up so we can go to Aunt Grace's before long. I'll be back."

They kept doing whatever they were doing as if I were the last thing on their mind. I made my way to the truck and spotted Victor out of the corner of my eye. I didn't want to acknowledge seeing him. I hated the way he made me feel—hated it and loved it at the same time. Just then my cell phone rang.

Saved by the bell. "Hello?"

"Yeah, sorry I was too busy to talk before. How long before you all arrive? I don't want the food getting cold while we wait for you."

It was just Grace, calling to give me all the details of the meeting as she made a point to throw off yet again about my staying at "that ritzy white-folk house." *This will only be the beginning*, I thought as I sped away from the inn. Getting together with them would give them one more opportunity to throw stones at me for whatever they thought I had done wrong now; from marrying that man from overseas, to never coming back home, to not having more than two words to say to the sorry lot in the past eight years. I guess they had some legitimate beefs, but I was going to stand my ground regardless. We'd sell the land, split the money, and go on our merry way, like we should have done when Daddy died.

Daddy's funeral was the typical Southern black funeral. The church was packed with family friends and nosey spectators from counties far and wide. Johnston Tayloe was such a well-known man that people felt right at home to not only come to the funeral, but back to the family house to gobble down as much Southern cooking as they could hold. I wished they'd all get the hell out of my daddy's house. I had lost my mama only three years earlier and now Daddy. My writing career was taking a beating and if one more fat, smelly black woman walked up in my face asking for more red velvet cake, I would throw the whole bunch out on their asses.

By the time the house cleared out from all the supposed mourners, the remaining Tayloe siblings would meet to talk about how to handle Andrew, the house, and Daddy's run-down Buick Regal. We all gathered in the living room of the family house and Grace started the meeting.

"Ya'll, I know this is not a good time to get into this stuff, but there ain't gonna be a better time. Andrew is still a minor and needs a guardian. I talked to Daddy about it before he died and let him know I would take care of Andrew."

We all nodded, expecting that announcement.

She continued. "As far as the house and car, I say we let this all sink in and talk about it in a few months when we can think straight."

"Dammit, Grace, why can't we just deal with it now? I don't have the strength to draw this mess out any longer," I heard myself say.

Everyone looked at me with shocked expressions. I wasn't sure where my attitude was coming from. Was it losing my daddy, the hot long funeral, the fat red velvet cake woman, or had I lost my mind?

As I think back on it now, there was just so much going on in my life, I had to take it out on someone, and so my brothers and sisters caught it. I was a failure at the one thing I thought I did well: writing. And now, both my parents were gone. Michael didn't get along with my family and somehow all this made me show my behind.

"I don't want nothing to do with this house or land and that car of Daddy's needs to go straight to the junk pile. I can't believe y'all gonna sit here and act like pure damn fools about this mess."

Again, they all looked shocked and no one spoke. They looked at me like I was some kind of stranger. I felt like a stranger even to myself. Where were the words coming from? After Bobby confronted me about my attitude, I lit into him and we all got so loud, Reverend Strippling had to come in and quiet us down. I wasn't sure where my anger was coming from but I couldn't stop it. I ran out of the room, grabbed Michael's hand, and told him to gather the kids so we could leave. Grace, Bobby, and Mabel followed me to the car, begging me to come back in and talk like rational adults.

"Come on, Bev, we can work this out, you're just stressed. We all are," Grace added, as Michael and I got into the car.

By the time we had all our stuff and the kids loaded into the car, I was too embarrassed by my actions to do anything except leave.

So that's how it happened. I left my home place eight years ago and even though some of the actual conversation is vague, I think I told my brothers and sisters to kiss my ass and I never wanted to see them again.

Did I mean it? I'm sure that when I said it, I meant some of it, but I'm not sure I meant never ever wanted to see them again. In fact I remember when I was picked up by my publisher and got my first six-figure deal, I wanted so bad to talk to Grace or see if Andrew needed anything for college. But I had burned that bridge and my pride wouldn't let me try to rebuild it.

So eight years later, I don't think any of us were sure what really happened that day, but we all knew it changed everything, forever. Grace had one version of what she heard me say, Bobby another. Mabel knew I got ugly with everyone, but she didn't seem to care; she still insisted on keeping the lines of communication open. I remember sitting in Melrose, between best-sellers, wondering why one of them didn't care enough about me to pick up the phone. My career was up and running. I had more money than a poor girl from Mississippi is supposed to get in a lifetime, so to hell with them. I convinced myself that I was better off without them. I didn't have to deal with the awkwardness of trying to make them understand Michael, and vice versa. No, it wasn't a bad setup, except the emptiness on special occasions when family usually surrounds you. After several years without them, it got easy to be without them. I forgot birthdays and special days that had anything to do with my family or Mississippi. The only reminder I had was the monthly conversation with Mabel. If it hadn't been for that, I would have been able to separate myself from them completely.

All the old memories were more than I could take, even with the mint juleps doing their work in my head. I'm not usually a sentimental person, but I wanted to visit my parents' grave site before World War III started with my siblings and me. Michael had warned me to keep my cool and not go in thinking the worst. He said things might actually be handled in a civil fashion and we could actually reestablish relationships and make a clean start of things. Yeah, right. He didn't know this bunch like I did. I knew they still blamed me for everything.

I pulled up to the cemetery and got out of the car feeling as strange as anyone who visits a cemetery alone in the middle of the day. It's not spooky or anything, just weird. What do you expect to accomplish coming to a huge gathering of dead people? We call it a visit, but visit usually implies a two-way exchange. You visit a friend in the hospital, a person in jail even, or perhaps a buddy you haven't seen in a while, but visit a dead person? I felt even more ridiculous as I approached the grave sites. Mama and Daddy's tombstones were right there where I left them eight years ago. A little weatherworn and not surrounded by flowers and mourners like I remember, but there they were just the same. Mama's gravestone had the title of her favorite song on it, "One Day at a Time." I smiled as I remembered Mama singing that song on more than one occasion. I guess trying to raise five children on a custodial-worker salary forced you to take it one day at a time. "One day at a time, sweet Jesus, that's all I'm asking from you. Just give me the strength to do every day what I have to do."

Mama was a religious woman and never played anything but gospel music in the house. Except that one time when Bobby was going to a Sadie Hawkins dance with Liz Bynum. That boy had been after Liz for months and when she asked him to that dance, that's all we heard about. Mama must have known how important it was for him to make a good impression because she actually let Bobby play "soul music" in her house. She let him practice the proper way to slow drag with a respectable girl. I can see it now. Mama in her wide, flowered dress and apron with chicken grease stains on the front, and Bobby still wearing his work clothes. Daddy found a station on the radio in the kitchen, the one we used when a bad storm knocked the power out. The song was "Tell It Like It Is" by Aaron Neville, and Mama and Bobby twirled around that kitchen as Grace and I teased him about trying to touch Liz's behind. That was the one and only time I ever saw my mama dance.

And then there was Daddy's gravestone. Two scriptures were engraved on it, as if one quote from the good book wasn't enough. That was another thing Grace and I got into it about. She had insisted on both scriptures, like Daddy was some kind of preacher or something. Since I was footing the bill for most of the funeral, I really didn't think she had the right to insist on spending more money. If the folks who visited Daddy's grave needed a Bible lesson, they should go to church, not the cemetery.

The more I looked down over the cement and grass, the sillier I felt. I was just about to turn around and end this meaningless encounter when someone tapped me on the shoulder.

"Oh, shit!" I yelled, as I spun around expecting to see Freddy Krueger or some horror movie character.

"Sorry, sis, I just—"

"Andrew, you know better than to sneak up behind someone in a cemetery, and you made me cuss in front of Mama and Daddy," I said, laughing.

With that Andrew grabbed me and we hugged like two long-lost lovers. We held on to each other for a while as if the physical contact would help us reconnect. I remembered where we were, so I let him go and looked around to make sure we were still alone.

"Sis, Grace called me at work to let me know you were in town. She said you were staying at Cedar, but I felt like you might make your way over here."

I didn't know what to say to him. Andrew was so grown-up-looking. It was only eight years, but my little brother was a man now. The last time I saw him, he was just a college student, and now he was a man with a career and all that.

"I thought it might be easier to see me first. You know how Grace and Bobby are—some things never change. I was hoping we could talk first before you confront the big guns."

"That's very civil of you, Andrew. I knew you would be the one to turn out with some good sense."

"The developers need a decision by tomorrow or they'll petition the state. We haven't talked in years and here we are having to make a major decision like this in a matter of a few hours."

"Andrew, what options do we have other than sell? It's the only thing that makes sense to me."

"Well, it's the easiest option and probably the one we'll end up going with, but, well . . ." He paused.

"What? Go ahead and say what's on your mind, son."

"One of us could develop it. I've done a little research and as long as we allow them to use the portion of the land they need for the road, we could develop the rest of it. We could find out what the EDC was planning to do with it and we could get the financing to do the same thing. If they were going to build apartments or condos, we could do that. And that way, the land would stay in the family." He sighed.

"They've gotten to you too. Andrew, how easy do you think it is to start a land development project? We all have jobs and responsibilities, and I, for one, have no intention of spending my best days in Vicksburg putting up houses so Old Man River can just tear them back down with one good, hard rain."

"Bev, it was just a thought. I know it seems crazy now, but if we'd started thinking about it when Daddy died, we could have done it. All it would have taken was a little working together. And think about it, working together was all we ever did on that land. The five of us kept the house clean, the grass and shrubbery cut and healthy, the garden groomed and productive. We've worked together before . . ." He paused again.

I could tell he was getting caught up in his own words. Andrew was just a little one, and the rest of us were the ones who worked together back then. And as he finished his thought, he knew it would take the rest of us to make anything good come out of this decision.

"Andrew, you're a good son. Mama and Daddy shoulda had you first instead of that ole jailbird Bobby."

"Come on, sis, Bobby has gotten some bad breaks. He's made his share of mistakes, but his biggest one is believing in this damn family too much. He doesn't have much going for him personally, so he keeps hope in you guys being as close as you were back then. It's all he has."

"Listen, Andrew, I know you mean well, but I can't live my life for Bobby and Mabel's shortcomings. If I do, I'll spend the rest of my life treading water in Mississippi just like Grace. And you had better watch yourself, before you end up trapped in this mediocrity."

"And I suppose you're so happy in Massachusetts having no ties to your own flesh and blood. How right is that, Bev? We were so much a part of your life, it has to create a void to be without us. None of us are perfect, but I sure as hell don't want to spend the rest of my life without any of you. Sometimes you don't know how much you need someone until they're gone," he concluded as he walked out of the cemetery, got into his car, and drove off.

I stood there wanting so much to be any place but at my parent's grave site. Andrew's words stung. I looked back down at the cement and grass and let the tears flow. "No, you don't know how much you need someone until they're gone."

I left the cemetery wondering what the reunion with the rest of them would be like. Andrew was the kind, easygoing one, and that hadn't gone well. The juleps were wearing off and I needed coffee and filters to take back to the suite. There was coffee in the main house, but in the morning, why stumble to the main house when you could have it conveniently in your room? I pulled up at a convenience store not too far from the inn, hoping not to see anyone who would recognize me. Seeing my family was already giving my nerves a workout.

As luck would have it, the first person I saw as I walked into the store was Benny Andrews—fat-ass Benny Andrews who used to live right down the road from us when we were kids. He was a greedy old man with only two teeth in his head and two dollars in his pocket. Used to always need to borrow something. And he knew when Mama was making pecan pie. It's like he had some kind of radar or something. Before Mama could get the pies out of the oven, Benny would come knocking on the door talking about the smell. He knew the right things to say to Mama:

"Miss Tayloe, you need to go in bidness wit these thangs."

"Now, Benny, you know nobody ain' gon pay money for dese pies."

"Miss Tayloe, I'd pay."

"Oh, you ain' got to pay, they'll be out in a minute. Rest yourself while they finish cookin' and I'll give you one to take home wit ya."

That's all that fool needed. He'd grin from ear to ear and wouldn't leave until he had a pie in hand and my mama blushing from all the compliments. I could tell he didn't recognize me. Eight years away saved me from having to deal with that fool. Maxwell House was the first thing I saw, so I grabbed a bag, a pack of filters, and got out of there before any other Vicksburg flashbacks walked through the door.

When I got back to the inn, Lisa and Junior had dressed and were ready to get over to Grace's to eat. They both looked a little nervous. They kept saying they were hungry, but I knew there was more to their antsy behavior. Lisa finally admitted she'd talked to Trey, and in his rundown of all the goodies Grace had prepared for our arrival, he also let her know Aunt Grace had a few words for her "high-minded, think-she-white sistah." The shit was most definitely about to hit the fan.

Chapter 11

As much as I dreaded walking into Grace's house, it was time. The two-day drive had all boiled down to this one event: dinner at Grace's followed by a meeting that would either settle the issue with the land and leave the Tayloe family in tact or tear us apart forever. All procrastinating aside, the moment of truth was upon us as we pulled up to the brick-ranch-style, single-family home Grace had lived in for more than twenty years. Not too much had changed since the last time I saw the place eight years ago. She still kept a nice flower bed in the front yard, and from the side view of the house, I could see a sizable garden in the backyard. There were at least six short rows of plants and weeds surrounded by wooden posts and chicken wire. I could see heads of lettuce peeking from the ground as if welcoming me home after a long journey. Although I couldn't see anything else in the garden, I was sure there were collards and cabbage plants with a few sideline items like cucumbers and tomatoes. I was sure we'd get a hefty portion of something from that garden.

I had stopped the truck, turned off the ignition, and removed the key before Lisa and Junior even started to stir. There was no eagerness in their strides as we walked toward the front door. I wondered if we should even go to the front door, since Grace always said, "The front door is for company, the side door is for family." I didn't feel much like family, so we kept heading toward the front door.

"Lord hamercy, Bev. How you doin', and Lord, look at these chiren," Mabel said, grabbing all three of us in one of her big ole arms.

"Hi, Mabel," I responded, as if talking to a new acquaintance instead of my own sister. Truth be told, Mabel was the main reason why I had made this ridiculous trip.

"Come on in dis house. Grace gon be glad to see y'all," she said, chuckling.

Grace was anything but glad to see us, but she covered it well as she reached one arm around me in a half-hug motion that communicated her true feelings to everyone except Mabel. The five of us stood there motionless for no more than five seconds, but it felt more like several minutes. The awkward tension was lost on Mabel.

"Grace, girl, you got this house smellin' up like you and Mama used to way back when," Mabel interjected amidst a wall of uncertainty and negative vibes.

"Well, we needed something to eat, didn't we?" Grace answered, without a smile.

We needed something to eat, but there was no way we needed the spread Grace had laid out on every available surface in the tiny kitchen/den combo. Mabel went to help Grace finish up whatever she was working on at the stove. Lisa and Junior spotted Trey, Mabel's son, in the yard, so they made their way out of that house in a hurry. I didn't exactly feel welcome in the kitchen, so I just made my peace to walk into the den area and scope out all the fixins until everyone else arrived.

Grace always did like putting on a show when mealtime came. That was only one of the things I couldn't really stand about her. I'm an okay cook, but Grace likes to throw her skills all up in your face. She makes so much food and won't stop cooking until everyone is ranting and raving about how good everything is and "nobody can cook 'so and so' quite like Grace."

Grace and Mabel continued working away in the kitchen as I took a spot in the den that would allow me to see clean through to the kitchen and living room. Grace was taking hot, golden fried chicken out of the pan while Mabel maneuvered around her, trying to get some homemade cheese biscuits out of the oven. The kitchen table was covered with large Pyrex dishes filled with collard greens decked out with a few pieces of smoked neck bones on top, fresh cabbage, string beans seasoned with leftover ham bone, lima beans and sweet peas. Most of the items were likely grown right in Grace's backyard. Grace got her gardening skills from Mama, who always said, "A garden is like a hand of provision reaching from deep beneath the soil to give life to all that partake." It took me years to go near the garden when I was a youngster, too afraid of some hand rising up from the ground.

Alongside the vegetables were baked yams covered with melted marshmallows, macaroni and cheese, and rice already smothered in gravy.

"I hope everyone likes gravy on their rice," I mumbled to myself as my sisters pranced around that tiny kitchen like two conductors leading an orchestra of country cooking.

There was hardly any room at the kitchen table for people to sit and eat. The bar area that divided the kitchen from the den was covered with all the meats. By now, Grace had added a large dish of the fried chicken to the other meats to complete the ensemble. There was sliced honey-baked ham, pork roast cut up North Carolina style, baked pork chops, pig's feet, barbecue ribs, chicken pastry with more pastry than chicken, and a pan of hot fried trout. That fool had been cooking the entire time I had been driving. Who did she think was gonna eat all that stuff? Just as I was about to shake my head in disgust, I saw the table in the living room lined with all kinds of cakes and pies. With my mouth still dropped open in shock, I turned around just in time to see Mabel pulling a home-made ice cream pie from the freezer.

"Bev, you member Grace's ice cream pie—ummm, dese thang is the bes," Mable continued, oblivious to the sweltering tension between Grace and me.

"Yes, Mabel, how could I forget?" I added, rolling my eyes, taking in the decor of the den.

Nothing is ever simple with Grace. Lacy pinks and baby blues covered every space of the tiny sitting area, which was neat and tidy, but with too many busy patterns for my taste. As my two sisters maneuvered around the kitchen, I shuffled my feet nervously over Grace's cheap knockoff Persian rug, laid delicately over a dull, aged hardwood floor that needed a good buffing. Beside the flower-decorated couch that looked like someone threw up flower petals all over it, there was a tapestry of more flowers hanging on the wall. I started getting dizzy as my eyes danced from the rug, to the couch, to the wall . . . flowers and noisy prints everywhere.

"You all right, Bev? you look tide."

"Yes, Mabel, I'm fine. I did just drive for two days. . . ."

"She just trying to show some concern. Don't bite her head off 'cause you surrounded by more good cooking than you've seen in eight long years," Grace snapped.

Just as I was about to give this long, tall, shapeless bitch a piece of my mind, Bobby and Andrew walked in with Bobby's baby mama and three nasty-nose illegitimate children in tow. Andrew greeted me as if we hadn't been hugging and crying together just an hour earlier. Bobby's baby's mama was pulling up the rear—all 300 pounds of her huffing and puffing as she climbed the four steps to the door. With her bleached-blond hair, bright red lipstick and skirt that belonged on someone half her size, she looked like something he found in a trailer park somewhere—trashy woman with a house full of children that Bobby had the nerve to think were all his.

"Hey, girl, dem kids of yours growed up nice-like," Bobby said with a chuckle as I hugged his neck. I almost gagged from the smell of the grocery store cologne he wore with pride, oblivious to the damage it must be doing to the environment. Andrew smiled behind Bobby's back, acknowledging my reaction to the smell. I reluctantly hugged his woman out of courtesy and because she was standing in the way as I made my way to the living room to check on the kids. When she pulled her left arm from around my neck, I noticed the brown crud lodged under her fake nails. She must not know the rule: you can't wear them if you can't maintain them. And goodness Lord, she has the stench of at least a couple days' accumulation of body odor. Bobby should have thrown a little of that cologne her way.

"Andrew, where is Chrissy? I told you to bring her so she could meet your long-lost sister," Grace added, loud enough for me to hear in the other room.

"I know, I know, but with what we need to talk about tonight, I just didn't think it was appropriate," Andrew replied, glancing through the doorway at me to gauge my reaction to Grace's rudeness.

"Ain't no need to let it get cold. I didn't cook all this food for it to sit here and look at us. Call the children in from outside and one of y'all boys ask the blessing," Grace demanded.

I went outside to get the kids while Bobby and Andrew went back and forth on who would ask the blessing. I wanted to add my two cents' worth, but being the outsider, I decided to just get the kids and keep my mouth shut. After we were all gathered in Grace's very hot little house, Bobby started with a prayer that no more went to the ears of God than one I would say. Amens rang out around the room as everyone started shuffling to get plates and pile on a little bit of everything.

After helping Lisa and Junior figure out what some of the food was, make their plates, and find a place for them to sit down, I started making my own plate. There was no way a little bit of everything would fit onto just one plate. As I took some fried chicken and collard greens, my mind drifted back to quarterly meetings at the family church years ago.

Mama and Grace had cooked for days, preparing for what ended up being about four cardboard boxes full of food. They started on Thursday night, cooking cakes and pies. The desserts alone would take up Thursday and most of Friday. After the cakes and pies were cooked and properly cooled, they sliced them and wrapped them in clear cellophane paper so all the church folk could see what kind of dessert they were getting. The trained quarterly meeting diner could easily tell you who cooked the dessert, just by looking at it through that cellophane paper.

Saturday morning started off with chopping collards and cabbage and a bunch of other vegetables from the garden. Then they boiled them in pots, rumbling on the stove until the kitchen was so hot, Grace and Mama had to cool themselves with ice water. Saturday night was for the meats. They baked ham and turkey, but saved the chicken frying for Sunday morning. I remember Daddy and Bobby loading the car with those boxes to take to the church. I don't really know how the quarterly meeting differed from any other service, except the service lasted longer than it should have, was more boring than usual, and . . . all that food!

If we had been wearing big floppy church hats and taking food out of cardboard boxes, I would have sworn I was at one of those church services.

"Bev, I know you're gonna eat more than that. Looks like you fell off some since last time we saw you," Grace added, strutting through the house like the "food police."

"Yes, Grace, I've lost a pound or two, but I've got to watch my girlish figure. We can't all naturally be skin and bones like you. Some of us have to watch what we eat," I replied to irritate her.

Grace hated for people to call her skinny, even though she practically disappeared when she turned sideways. She gave me a piercing look that meant I had better leave it with that comment and not take it a step further. So I did, until Bobby had to open his mouth and show his ignorance.

"No, we ain't all alike, but at least everybody 'round here know we family, even though you up in the city kissin' dem white-folk ass and won't even use yo' real name. You ain't nobody, Beverly Bradford Dunn. You jus' another Mississippi nigga runnin' from who you is," Bobby lashed out, getting closer to my face with each word.

By the time he finished his say, the kids were out of the kitchen and headed back outside, knowing full well this was getting ugly in a hurry.

"You got some nerve, Bobby Tayloe, or should I call you by the number that's permanently etched across your criminal behind," I returned, not backing down from him one bit.

"Stop it, you two! We didn't come here to jump into each other's stuff. We got decisions to make and we don't have a lot of time," Andrew said, pushing us apart.

Our display seemed to make everyone lose their appetites, so Grace and Mabel started putting food away and clearing off the table so we could talk about what we really were there for, before somebody got a piece taken out of his ass.

I couldn't believe my own brother had gone there, claiming I am running from who I really am. He has no idea why I wrote the stuff I wrote. And my pen name has nothing to do with them, but he's not even worth the breath it would take to explain it all.

"I guess that uppity husman of yours couldn't take time off his important work to drive you down here to clear up dis mess. What in the world made you want to marry up with one of dem anyway, you know dey into voodoo." Bobby went there again, and I had had all I was gonna take from him.

"Listen, fool, I know you aren't questioning my choice in a mate, when you don't even have the decency to marry this trashy stank ho you're with. And don't tell me you think all them babies are yours. . . . Any fool knows the one with green eyes didn't come from your gene pool," I added, not knowing if Bobby was going to punch me or what.

Andrew, Grace, and Mabel interrupted this time, pulling us apart and trying to get things under control again. Bobby glanced over at the baby with the green eyes like it was the first time he'd noticed that boy looked half white. Andrew pulled me into the living room while Grace, Mabel, and Bobby stayed in the kitchen putting food away.

"Sis, this isn't going in the right direction. Bev, you gotta see that Bobby is attacking you because he doesn't know what else to do with what he's feeling. In his own way, he's questioning your writing under a pen name because he really wants to be associated with you. We are all proud of your accomplishments and we would love to say, 'That's our sister,' regardless of what you're writing about. Bobby just wants to know that you and Michael accept him with all his faults. Bev, you're the educated one, you have to be able to see what's really going on here," Andrew said softly so the others couldn't hear him.

When did my baby brother get so damn smart? I knew he was right, so I just nodded my head and sat back to let my temper cool down before I tried to make my way back into the lion's den. I assumed I would catch it from Grace first. I had no idea Bobby was going to lay into me the way he had.

"Jesus, I wonder what Grace has in store for her long-lost sister," I mumbled as I closed my eyes and let my head fall back on the stiff Victorian chair, wondering what the hell I had been thinking two days ago when I decided to return to Vicksburg, Mississippi, after being separated from my brothers and sisters for eight years.

Chapter 12

So, after too many years apart and two days of agitated travel, the situation was going from bad to worse. My fight with Bobby about the paternity of his children got the kids' attention outside. As I sat in Grace's living room trying to cool down, Lisa peeked her head in the door to see if the coast was clear.

"Ma, can we go to the store? Trey says it's right up the street and I promise we'll come straight back," she pleaded.

I knew she just wanted to get away from the scene she had witnessed. "Sure, go ahead, but just that one store, nowhere else—your daddy already told you about driving on the interstate, so stay right here in this area. Don't let Trey and Junior get you into trouble. You're the only one with a license, so please be careful—and come straight back, Lisa," I yelled as she dashed back out the door, only half acknowledging my words.

She would be fine. Besides, I had bigger fish to fry with these fools who called themselves my family. Ten years ago, if anyone would have told me I'd be fighting like junkyard dogs with my oldest brother, I'd just laugh. We were all so close once. I couldn't imagine fighting about something as simple as the place we all called home. Rich, arrogant people who hadn't been raised right were the ones who fought over land, not a poor black family who grew up living off the land, reaching out to help others and doing good in the community. My parents would flip over twice in their graves if they knew we were acting up like this over something we all poured our heart and soul into. I wanted to hit the rewind button and go back to a time so long ago and start over. But you can't go back. There was no starting over, only moving forward. And moving forward was the hardest thing to do, considering the four people in the other room felt like strangers to me and not my own flesh and blood.

One of the strangers joined me in my reflection. Andrew came back into the living room, since the others were still putting the food away.

"Bev, why didn't Michael come with you, if you don't mind talking about it?"

"No, Andrew, I don't mind talking about it, but it's kind of complex really, and since you're not married, it probably won't make much sense to you."

"Well, try me anyway, Sis."

He handed me a glass of iced tea with plenty of lemon slices swimming around in the sweet mixture of caffeine and water. I sipped the tea, almost reluctant to get into it with Andrew.

"Michael and I came to an agreement about family issues. You see, years ago, we both tried to do everything together, like a happy couple."

"Well, isn't that the way it's supposed to work?"

"In theory it is. When you get married, you are a team, partners in crime, you make decisions together, but what you soon learn is that blood is thicker than water."

"Oh, yeah, in what way?"

I sipped my tea, realizing I was already into it, with no way to turn back now. He genuinely wanted to know why I made the trip alone, why I needed to fight this battle by myself.

"In the way brothers and sisters don't want outsiders telling them what to do with their family stuff. Brothers and sisters know each other and can look over one another's mess. You know, the way we all covered for Bobby when he was getting into so much trouble and dropping babies all over town. And the way we all pitched in to help Mabel when she had Trey and that fool left her. Brothers and sisters do that for each other."

"Yeah, I see."

"Well, Michael's people are from Haiti, so most of the drama in his family is thousands of miles away. We don't get the opportunity to get mixed up in what's going on with the Lamarks. That's a fortunate thing, actually. With my family, it was just the opposite. From day one, Michael and I both tried to attend all the family functions and make all the Tayloe family decisions together. It never worked out right. It was always either Michael and Grace or Michael and Bobby arguing about who had the right to say what we should do. And I'm not talking about big stuff like family land. I'm talking about little simple messes. Michael, being the man in my life, wanted to represent me in family decisions, but it didn't sit well with Grace and Bobby. They always wanted to know what say he had since he was just an 'in-law.'"

"I remember some of the yelling matches," he said with a giggle. "Kind of feels like what's going on today. So what did you and Michael decide?"

"Michael leaves things regarding my family up to me. He stays out of it, at least away from the forefront. When we were making decisions at Daddy's funeral, he stayed in the background. When you and Grace called about the house getting condemned, he told me to do whatever I wanted. He gives me his opinions and then leaves it up to me. Same thing about the land now. He gives me the freedom to do whatever I think is necessary. He stays out of it in order to keep the peace. It should be better this way. Family should be able to relate to family, especially when you take out all the outside influences. Michael never quite understood all the times we bailed Bobby out of the messes he kept getting into, but he's not supposed to understand. That's my brother and I can bad-mouth him, but I don't want anyone else to low-rate him, you know?"

"Yeah, I know exactly what you're talking about. So, is it working, your little setup for handling family stuff?"

"You tell me. After the outburst we just had, I don't think it's done much good. I don't seem to be handling it very well on my own."

"I wouldn't beat myself up about it if I were you. At least you're here now, that's got to count for something, right?"

I nodded my head and finished my tea as he continued.

"Well, I think part of the problem is just not talking about it all those years. Not giving everyone a fair and equal say in the matter. I just hate that so many years have passed, and now we have our backs against the wall. I still say we could have done something productive with that land to keep it in the family. I still believe that's what Daddy would have wanted. But, anyway, no more delaying. The EDC needs to hear from us by tomorrow. And now we have decisions to make, before there's any bloodshed," he joked as we got up to join the others.

I reluctantly shuffled back into the kitchen, trying not to make eye contact with anyone. This had to be done. It was only a few acres of land, but we had to make a call. I'd heard of families fighting over just about anything and everything, from a little shack of a house worth no more than a couple thousand dollars, to an old end table. I chuckled as I imagined the end table Mama had had handed down to her from her mother. It leaned to one side because one of the legs had lost the little knobby part on the bottom. The table was scratched and scuffed from years of coffee cups and pencil marks. But Mama wouldn't get rid of it. She pitched a fit every time Daddy tried to throw it out. I imagined the little worthless table getting destroyed in the flood and a depressing feeling washed over me. It doesn't matter how large or small the thing, it's about the worth attached to it by the owner. Andrew's words rang back in my ears,

"We could have done something. . . . That's what Daddy would have wanted." But it was too late. Too much time had passed, with too many words unspoken, and too many bad words spoken. I watched Mabel and Grace still moving through that little kitchen with skilled accuracy, wrapping and packing bowls and pans. I wanted to join them, but pride held me back. Pride wouldn't let my feet move or my heart soften.

Chapter 13

Bobby and Andrew were in the den talking about the baseball strike and I had a headache setting in that had Bobby's name all over it. I glanced down at my watch and realized the kids had been gone at least an hour and should be getting back soon. Everyone was distracted so I went into one of Grace's bedrooms to call Michael.

Bobby's makeshift family occupied the first room I walked into. His woman was feeding the baby, and I wanted to go in and wipe his nasty nose, since he seemed to be getting more snot in is mouth than Enfamil. I apologized for the disturbance and closed the door behind me.

The second room must've been Grace's room because it was laid out just like Grace, all frills and no substance. I grabbed one of the fluffy pillows off the bed and ran my hand over the print. A gorgeous needlepoint pillow with a brilliant magnolia etched in the center, surrounded by a braided tassel trim. I smiled at Grace's mix of class and clutter as I dialed the number.

"Hi, honey. You miss me?" I asked, trying not to sound like the same woman who had been enjoying the company of another man hours earlier.

"I guess they haven't tarred and feathered you yet, since you were able to make this call," he joked.

"They've tarred me all right, and I'm not sure I'll stick around for the feathering part," I added, knowing full well he'd want an explanation, but I had no time to give one. "Before you start with the questions, be assured I have it all under control. I'll call you when I get back to the inn tonight with the details. I think I hear Andrew calling me," I lied.

"Wait, how are the kids?"

"They are kids, adapting much better than I am, but then again they ran out when the heat got turned up."

"What?"

"I gotta go, I'll call later. Love ya. Andrew, I'm coming," I yelled, still hanging up the phone, leaving Michael in the dark.

As I walked back up the short hallway that led to the front part of the house, I glanced to my right and caught a glimpse of the Leroy room. Since the others were occupied, I decided to peek in and see if the room still looked like it did eight years ago. The door was slightly cracked open, enough for me to recognize the room, but not quite enough for me to see the contents. I eased the door open, hoping Grace was too involved in her busy work to hear me invading her privacy. The room had a nice fragrant smell, not like the rest of the house. All the other rooms smelled like Grace had been cooking for three days, but this room smelled clean and fresh—no fried chicken scent or the sour smell of collard greens. This room was almost like a room in another house. It seemed separate from all the other goings-on that made up Grace's meager existence. This room was stuck in time, although it had an up-to-date energy. The bed was the central focus of the room, with a basic comforter in a modest print. Nothing like the rest of Grace's things. The decor had a masculine feel to it, kind of like Leroy was still using the room, but only for an occasional weekend visit. The dresser and small nightstand by the bed were the ones Mama gave Grace when she first moved out and got this house. The Leroy furniture was gone. Why was the furniture not there? Was this a message? Was Grace finally moving on? I didn't have time to look for clues and nose around anymore. Andrew actually was calling me this time.

"We need to go ahead and sit down and talk through what options we have and how we will proceed tomorrow with the development people," Andrew began with the same level head he had used earlier when he pulled Bobby off me.

We had all gathered in Grace's den, ready to have a civilized adult conversation. Andrew strategically positioned us so that if something erupted between Bobby and me or Grace and me, he could get to us before anyone got hurt.

"Here are the facts given to me by the Economic Development Commission for Vicksburg and Warren County. They would like to buy the entire fifteen acres outright for seventy-five thousand dollars. Daddy only paid two thousand for the land when he bought it, so that's not a bad sale price. It's riverfront property so they want to develop it as such, but the front portion of the property will be used to add another highway, so traffic going to the mini-mall and Lexingham condos and all that stuff will not bottleneck. You know how traffic is in that area in the mornings and evenings when folks are going to and from work."

Everyone sat still, only nodding occasionally as Andrew continued presenting the facts.

"Our only other option is to divide the land and sell only the portion they need for the road. We could still keep the portion near the river only if we agree to develop it and not just leave it as an empty spot like it is now. If we do nothing, the commission will petition the state and show just cause as to why they need the land and then we'll have to deal directly with the state and that might not be such a good thing. State officials aren't always as patient and forgiving as these commission people that we live near and work with every day. So what do you say?"

No one said a word. I hadn't planned to speak first, so I just looked around the room, wondering what intelligent thing Bobby would come up with. Or would Grace have the balls to speak her mind, if she even knew how. It shocked us all when Mabel spoke up.

"Y'all, I know I ain' really got no bidness sayin' nuthin', but dat was my daddy land too and I jes hate dat we gon sit back and watch dem do God knows what to it and probly make a whole lot a money doin' it. Y'all member how hard Daddy worked fo dat lan? Member how he came home every day, talkin' 'bout what dey doin' now? Y'all member, right?"

We all nodded our heads yes, so Mabel would continue.

"Well, I know we got to sell it, but mo than I hate dat we got to sell it, I hate dat we ain' friends no mo. We brother and sisters, so we sho ought to at leas be friends. We can't do nothin' 'bout the lan now, but y'all know Mama and Daddy ain' raise us to act like dis. I know dat much and my mind ain' all dat clear all de time."

I could feel the tears in my eyes as Mabel made more sense than she ever had. She surprised us all and when she finished talking, you could hear a pin drop in the room.

I sat there thinking about what she had said. She was right. Once upon a time, we would do anything for each other and one Tayloe couldn't move two steps without a brother or sister being right there. For some reason all I could think about was the time Bobby almost bled to death.

We were just kids, but Bobby had gotten it into his head that he was some kind of daredevil or something. He took a wood plank from Daddy's storage barn and propped it up on a cement block. Grace, Mabel, and I sat there watching him, just like it was some kind of TV show. He got onto his bike and rode far enough back to get a good start. He pedaled harder and faster until he got right up on the plank, and then he went airborne. He landed a few feet out into the yard and we all started cheering. Our reaction took the daredevil show to a new level. Bobby was convinced he could accomplish a "greater feat," as he called it. We sat there waiting to see what he would do next. This time he repositioned the plank and block and set some old bottles and cans out in front of the makeshift ramp. The bottles and cans represented a greater risk, but none of us, including Bobby, saw how close he was to the tree. He pedaled that little bike and this time when he hit the ramp and went airborne, he came down right up against that tree. His head hit first and blood splattered everywhere. Grace was close enough to get some on her dress. We all started screaming, thinking Bobby was dead or close to it. Mama came running out of the house, yelling for Daddy with every step. They grabbed the bloody, unconscious body and we all jumped into the car and made our way to the hospital. They took Bobby back to some room and hours seemed like days as they worked on him. He suffered a minor concussion and was left with one nasty scar on his nose. For most of his teenage years, he got teased about the scar, but wouldn't you know that by the time he graduated from high school, that scar was his trademark. Girls said it made him look kind of dangerous, like he had been in a knife fight or something. He had a perfect face, perfect smile, charm and charisma, and one scar that made the whole package more appealing.

I smiled at the irony as Bobby jolted me back to reality when he made up an excuse about checking on his kids. Andrew just sat there flipping through the paperwork from the development commission. And Grace—Grace was staring at me with a look of contempt that sent chills down my spine.

"What the hell is your problem?" I asked.

"You're ready to just get this day over with, sell the land, get your money, and go back to your life in Melrose, aren't you? You didn't hear a word Mabel said, did you?"

"I heard Mabel and what she said was sweet, but we have business to attend to. This isn't some damn family reunion for Christ's sake. We should've made this decision right after Daddy died or at least after the flood destroyed the house, but no, you and Andrew just put a Band-Aid over it, hoping that a little fried chicken, collard greens and sappy talk would make everything all right. Well, business is business, Grace, and you can't let things go undealt with."

"You have some nerve talking about dealing with stuff. What you been doing? Hiding out for years ain't exactly dealing with stuff, now, is it? You can sit up there with all your society friends and look down your pious nose at us country folk, but you aren't any better than we are. Money doesn't make you somebody, Beverly, or should I call you Mrs. Dunn. We're tired of you looking down on us because we're simple people who like a simple life. There's nothing wrong with who we are. And we will not carry on like we're walking on eggshells just so we won't offend your nappy-headed husband. Michael is so quick to say we don't accept him, but I don't see him down here trying to 'deal with stuff,' as you put it." Grace was almost out of breath and coming out of her seat as she finished her spill. "If you couldn't be a part of this family for all these years, I'm not sure you should even get a say in what happens with that land."

"I'm sorry if I prefer handling things differently than you all. And I would appreciate it if you ignorant bastards would leave my husband out of this. This is not about him."

"To hell it isn't. He had so much to say when Daddy died. He was gonna get one of his friends to help us settle the estate for free. All big talk from a big-time nigger. I'm still not sure what you ever saw in that fool."

"Oh, and I suppose Leroy was the perfect man." It slipped out of my mouth before I could catch it. I didn't mean to go there. That was too far and even I knew it.

Grace started crying as Bobby, Andrew, and Mabel stared at me in disbelief. Everyone had been so careful not to bring up Leroy. I didn't know how to get the words back. The different furniture in the room had been Grace's way of trying to move on. She had tried to put that part of the past in the past. But in just a few seconds I brought it all back. I hadn't meant to mention Leroy . . . anything but Leroy. I knew how much she loved him, and he loved her, until his last breath. A woman could only dream of that kind of love. I had only dreamed of that kind of love.

Grace bit back the tears and came right back at me. We were toe-to-toe yelling at the top of our lungs. I tried to walk away from her, but she grabbed me just as I got into the living room. I snatched away from her and opened the front door before I did something I would regret.

"Oh, so you gonna walk out again? How long you gonna be gone this time, Mrs. Dunn?"

With every bit of strength in my body I turned around and back-handed Grace so hard, I was certain I had slapped the taste out of her mouth. As Andrew grabbed me and shoved me outside, I saw blood trickling from the corner of Grace's mouth. I knew I had crossed the line, but it felt good to let it all come out.

Chapter 14

I should have known Grace was not going to let me get away with slapping the mess out of her, and she didn't. Before I could get my bearings and explain to Andrew that I was leaving, she came bursting out the front door and dove right on my back. There we were, like a couple of kids, rolling around in her front yard shouting obscenities at each other. Bobby and Andrew were doing their best to pull us apart, but Grace had a grip on my ponytail and if they separated us, I would certainly lose a patch of hair.

That bitch. I was just about to punch or kick her or do something to make her let go of my hair, but Bobby got her hand away from my head and Andrew pulled me away from her. We both finally got back onto our feet, winded and still mad as hell.

"Grace, I can't believe you did some ghetto shit like that," I yelled.

"Me? You disrespect my house and slap me and then have the nerve to say I'm the one acting ghetto?" she returned.

By now neighbors were on their front porches getting an eyeful of all the Tayloe family losing their freaking minds. They had long been speculating that our family was in crisis when they stopped seeing me at family gatherings. Grace had to make up a different lie every holiday to cover it up. And now, seeing Grace and I tussling like schoolchildren right in her front yard, they knew the Tayloe family had some real problems. It had gotten about as bad as I thought it could get, when I saw the two police cars pull into Grace's yard like they were going to the scene of a barroom brawl. The officers jumped out, asking for the owner of a white Lexus truck. By now, neighbors had left their porches and boldly walked right up into Grace's yard to find out what was going on. I looked in the driveway for the first time and realized my truck wasn't there. The kids still weren't back and it had been nearly three hours. My truck isn't white, but it is a Lexus, so I raised my hand toward the officer like a schoolchild anticipating a scolding.

"Ma'am, we need to speak with you," one officer stated as he guided me toward the police car.

For the first time since all the craziness started, I realized the kids weren't back and I could feel all the blood leaving my face. There was something wrong with the kids. It had to be something bad for the officers to come to the house to find us.

"Ma'am, we need to get you inside. You need to come with us."

Grace and Bobby were yelling at the officer, trying to figure out what was going on. The officers were asking questions about my truck and what the kids were wearing. I couldn't even remember my own name, much less what they had on. So much was happening so fast. I tried to remember what Lisa was wearing. Had she changed her clothes before we left for Grace's? Junior was wearing jeans, always jeans. I thought he was wearing a red T-shirt, but I wasn't sure. I couldn't think with the sirens blaring in my ear and the officers rushing me to the police car. Andrew handed me my purse, and I got into the police car, motioning for Mabel, and still trying to figure out what was going on. I knew what was going on. A mother knows. But I wanted someone to tell me something, anything, to assure me this wasn't what I thought it was.

"We only need the owner of the truck, ma'am. You can come with the others," an officer told Mabel.

122

"Her son was in the truck too. This is my sister!" I yelled, wanting Mabel in the car beside me—wanting *someone*.

"We're sorry, ladies, but there has been an accident. It happened about an hour ago. We're taking you to the scene now. It's just up the road a piece. Some of the locals said it looked like the truck they saw at this house earlier tonight. That's how we found you. Are you sure you don't remember what your kids were wearing?"

"Are they okay? What happened? Are they at the hospital?" I was rapid-firing questions at the officer without answering any of his.

Mabel still hadn't said a word.

"We need to make sure the kids are okay. Can't we just go to the hospital first? I need to see my kids."

"I think they airlifted the occupants of the vehicle to Warren County Hospital, and we'll get you ladies there as soon as possible."

Those words were still ringing in my ear, or maybe it was the sirens: "There has been an accident . . . airlifted to the hospital." I had had nightmares about something like this from the time Lisa started driver's education. Nothing good ever comes after the words, "there's been an accident," especially not when there are teenagers involved.

Mabel still wasn't speaking. I reached for her hand. She was crying silently. I wanted to be strong for her, but I needed all the strength I could muster to deal with my own fears.

Within minutes we were approaching a section of road with lights flashing everywhere. Curious motorists had pulled over to get a better look. The police car came to a stop and we all got out. I grabbed Mabel's arm and screamed as I spotted it lodged up under the front of a big rig. It was my truck.

The officer was talking, but there was so much noise. I knew the kids had to be in pretty bad shape. The top had been ripped off the truck, and I could tell the front compartment had been crushed.

"We've got to get to the hospital! I need to see my kids!" I cried hysterically.

"Let's go, Bob. She's given us a positive ID on the vehicle," one officer said to the other.

"Yeah, you're right. This is unit twenty-nine, we have a positive on the vehicle in that ten twenty-two PI on Ramsdale Road. Copy."

"Roger that," a voice echoed from the walkie-talkie.

"Unit twenty-nine en route to Warren County Hospital . . . Twenty-nine out."

As we drove away from the scene, I got a better view of my truck. I could see the back door on the passenger side lying in a ditch. I remembered the day I bought that truck: a golden pearl Lexus LX 470, ivory leather interior with California walnut trim. I remembered the salesman giving a long spiel about the safety features, but all I cared about was the luxury features and the DVD player and navigation system. I took it home and Lisa and Junior sighed because I didn't get a "cool car."

I remembered Lisa getting her driver's license in that truck. And most recently, I remembered the night we were robbed in that truck. I could still hear Lisa's whimpering as we tried to find a place to stop for the night. *My babies.* The tears started rolling and I was sure they'd never stop.

Just as I was about to turn away from the scene, I spotted the driver of the big rig. He was talking to the policemen and waving his arms like he was re-creating the accident for them. His hands were shaking and he was clearly out of breath.

What is he saying? I was thankful when Mabel gripped my arm. I wasn't alone. I put my arms around her to offer my support, but mainly to get my eyes off the scene that would no doubt be permanently etched into my memory. There were people all along the road, looking at the mangled truck and trying to get the latest on what had happened to whom. I could feel the breath leaving my body as if I were hyperventilating. I opened my mouth wider, trying to take in more air. I felt like I was gasping, but no more air would come in. I wanted to roll down the window, but I couldn't find the handle. My eyes wouldn't focus on anything but the image of my kids who desperately needed me. I gasped harder and just closed my eyes, still holding Mabel's hand with a tight grip to let her know I was there, to let me know she was there, neither of us was alone.

Before I knew it, we were pulling up to the hospital emergency entrance. The car came to a screeching halt and both officers jumped out, opening our door and motioning for us to get out. There was an ambulance just in front of the police car, and then just a few hundred feet away, I saw the helicopter. I jumped as another police car swerved into the curved driveway behind us. I could see Andrew, Bobby, and Grace getting out as someone called my name.

"Mrs. Lamark, over here," a voice called from a room just inside the emergency doors. I walked into the room to a man in a white doctor's coat. I know doctors have to be trained better than this man demonstrated. Bad news was plastered all over his face. With my hands shaking and my knees giving way under my weight, I tried to walk toward him to hear whatever was causing his face to contort like he had just tasted something sour.

"My God, no!" I remember yelling, as everything went black.

When I came to, I was in a small room with a few couches and chairs, a TV set, and a phone on the wall. I looked around the room at my brothers and sisters. Mabel just sat in the corner looking lost. Bobby was stroking the back side of her hand, like he was comforting a small child. Andrew leaned in close to me and began to speak.

"Bev, the accident was pretty bad. They're gonna take you in to see Lisa as soon as you're ready," he choked as he let the words tumble from his mouth.

"I want to go now!" I yelled, grabbing on to the arm of the chair to pull myself up.

"I know, Bev, and she wants to see you too, but . . ."

"And where is Junior? I need to get to him, too," I continued, pulling away from Andrew. I noticed that the others were staring at me, like they knew something I did not. "Where is Junior, dammit?" I yelled, trying not to let my mind think about the fact that Andrew had only mentioned Lisa.

Andrew begged me to take a seat. The scene was nothing like the movies where the mother walks in to find out that her child didn't make it. There were no caring doctors and sympathetic nurses to break the news to me. Only my family and a deep pain that shot through my body with such force, I was sure it was what shoved me to the floor. I wasn't out but a minute before Grace and Bobby were pulling me back to the chair I had just gotten up from.

Andrew went on to tell me that the cops had called the Melrose police department and they were sending someone over to tell Michael. "They're gonna get him to the airport and on the next flight out tonight."

The next few hours felt like they were happening off somewhere in the distance, like watching a black and white movie. I watched as Grace, Bobby, and Andrew went in and out of the waiting room door. They talked, but I couldn't connect the words. They weren't talking to me. At some point the black and white figures took on color again and I felt a hand on my shoulder. Representatives from the police department and the hospital sat down with me to tell me what they knew so far. They let Andrew stay with me and the others left. They told me that Lisa apparently had been driving and Trey was in the passenger seat. They assume Junior was in one of the backseats, but not wearing a seat belt, because his body had been thrown toward the front of the vehicle. After the vehicles made contact, the truck lodged under the front grill of the rig and was dragged another hundred feet as the driver of the rig tried to stop. According to the driver of the rig and several witnesses, my truck crossed the center line and slammed head on into the eighteen-wheeler. Apparently they hadn't seen the rig, or had spotted it too late. Lisa and Trey survived, Junior did not. They cruised over the words like they were just any words, not nouns and verbs ripping at my heart.

As the two people were talking, I looked around the room waiting for someone to tell me this wasn't happening. I waited for something to wake me up from this nightmare. I wanted this lady to stop talking about maximum speed and skid marks and tell me my babies were okay. This couldn't be happening. These kinds of things happen to other people. Nothing this bad could be happening to me, not now.

The thoughts were more than I could handle. This lady was still rambling on and I was sure there was a mistake. When she finally paused, I asked if they had any idea what caused the accident. Lisa was such a careful driver.

"Mrs. Lamark, we're not sure what caused your daughter to veer into the other lane. Your daughter is hurt pretty badly. We didn't want to make her any more uncomfortable. But we speculate the accident had something to do with the fact that her blood-alcohol level was—"

"Alcohol!" I yelled. "Where the hell did they get alcohol?"

Chapter 15

When I finally walked into Lisa's room, I had calmed myself enough to not let the shock of hearing that she'd been drinking show. Lisa's eyes were closed, and as I walked to her bed, I didn't know what to feel. I wanted to grab her and hug her tight. And part of me was still aching for Junior. I wanted to be a good mother and put aside the hurt and attend to the child that was alive and needed me. I stood over her bed, shaking my head, and trying to figure it out, when Lisa opened her eyes.

She didn't speak. I didn't know what to say either. The nurse walked in and nodded her head as if giving me the okay to move closer to Lisa. So, since there were no words stirring in my heart, I crawled onto the big bed beside my baby and held her. I held and rocked, never wanting her to be out of my sight again.

I'm sorry, Ma, it was all my fault," she cried.

I held her tighter, not wanting her to feel the guilt and remorse I felt for being so irresponsible. Lisa had faired best of all three kids. Both of Trey's legs were broken and he had some internal bleeding that they were able to get a handle on soon after they got him to the hospital. The nurse had told me that most of Lisa's injuries were emotional. Besides the scrapes and bruises on her face and forearms from the air bag deploying, she was okay. Her body started quaking as she sobbed and begged me to forgive her. I couldn't respond to her through my own tears. They had put Lisa in one of the short-term holding rooms in Emergency. There wasn't much privacy on that hall since people were coming and going all the time. As the noise level rose and fell outside the door, we held each other, letting our souls groan for such a loss on a late Thursday night and the void that would be with us for a lifetime.

"Lisa, I'm gonna go, you need some rest. We've got to get you feeling better. They're gonna keep you here tonight, just for observation. Your father is on his way. Your aunts and uncles are all here and Trey is going to be fine. A few broken bones, but he's going to be okay, and so will you, so just relax," I said, stroking her hair and laying my chin on top of her head.

I didn't want her to see my eyes. I didn't want her to know I was so hurt. I couldn't let her blame herself any more than she already was. So, I lay there trying to convince her that everything would be okay. The lies seemed to bounce around the four pale white walls as the noise level outside the door rose again. She shook her head as if hoping I was right, all the while knowing nothing would ever be the same.

The nurse came in and whispered that I should let her get some rest. I took that as my cue to leave. I started to go to Trey's room. I hadn't seen him yet. They told me the doctors had been with him ever since the chopper landed with his battered and broken body. They said he hadn't been wearing his seat belt and faced much of the same impact that Junior had faced. Only Trey lived. *Who gets to decide who lives and who dies?*

I wondered this as I passed the door to Trey's room, only peeking in to see a bed surrounded by white lab jackets. I had seen the truck. It was a wonder any of them survived. I made my peace to take it one step at a time. Junior's death, Lisa drinking, and Trey's injuries.

As I tried to mumble reassuring thoughts to myself, they kept getting caught in my throat, making me want to gag.

I went back to the waiting room where Andrew was sitting with my purse on his lap and his eyes glued to a picture on the wall—a picture of a little boy, no more than six, sitting in a swing with a smile that stretched from ear to ear. The caption was something about giving blood. Andrew stared, but I knew he wasn't seeing a thing on the picture.

By the time I left the hospital, it was nearly 1:00 in the morning. Mabel was so out of it, they suggested she stay overnight for observation. A male nurse, older and caring, gave her a sedative and assured me that she would be just fine until morning, when the light of day would bring this ugly mess to plain view again. I asked Andrew to take me back to the inn. It seemed like the right thing to do, although I certainly didn't want to go back there alone. It would be at least a few more hours before Michael arrived, and I needed someone close by to comfort me when the reality got too intense. By the time Andrew pulled into the inn parking lot, I realized that Grace and Bobby were tagging along.

"I hope you don't mind, Bev, they wanted to come too. No one seems to want to be alone right now. Maybe we can all stay with you until Michael gets here. It might do you some good," Andrew suggested.

"That's fine, Andrew, I need the company."

After a few awkward seconds of eye contact with Grace and Bobby, I motioned for them to follow us to the suite. I remember opening the door and walking in, trying to find some light. When I finally stumbled over a coffee table and clumsily bumped against the sofa, I located a lamp. The sixty watts of light made the room almost too bright. I had been in that bright, loud hospital for so long and then the deep dark, deafening quiet of the car, the light almost pierced my eyeballs. Through tear-stained, mascara-smeared eyes, I looked around the room. Junior had left his socks and shoes lying in the middle of the floor, knowing full well I told him to always put his things away. He always argued that he would be back for them and they were fine right where he left them. Lisa had left her Walkman lying on the sofa. No doubt it was still tuned to the station she was listening too when I returned from the grave site earlier today. And then I spotted a bottle cap on the floor near the kitchenette. I slowly walked toward it, afraid to find out what it was. Beer. The bottle cap was all that remained of the beer—the beer that blurred Lisa's judgment just enough to cause her to veer a little too much over that center line.

I couldn't bring myself to ask Lisa about the drinking. When the nurse first mentioned the blood-alcohol level, I almost wanted to give her a piece of my mind. But now the proof was staring me right in the face. The kids had been experimenting, like teenagers do, wanting to act like adults. But adults don't always set the right example. They had apparently been back at the inn while their parents were acting like children who needed a good spanking. They drank alcohol and then got back into the truck and attempted to come back to Grace's house as if nothing had happened. But something had happened. Something terrible had happened.

"Bev, Michael just called from the airport. A police escort is there to pick him up and they are bringing him straight over here," Grace reported.

What time is it? Grace sensed my confusion and handed me my watch. I was glad she went on to tell me it was 2:00 in the morning, because I was having a time getting my eyes to adjust. The sixty watts were still shining way too brightly. After taking a few minutes to get myself together, I asked if anyone had checked on Mabel.

"She needs someone too. Why are you all here? She's in no condition to see about Trey on her own and she doesn't have a husband rushing to be by her side. Why did you guys leave her alone?"

"Bev, Mabel had an episode at the hospital. You were out cold then," Andrew answered.

"Is she going to be okay?" I begged. Not another tragedy, I prayed.

"She gon be fine, Bev, you know how she have dem spells. She jus had one a dem, dat's all. Dey gon watch her and prob'ly send her home tomorrow and den we'll be wit her," Bobby explained.

I knew what spell Bobby was talking about. It's actually a form of epileptic seizure, but it doesn't knock her out or anything. She just kind of blanks out when something is too stressful. Her brain overloads and just shuts down temporarily. I remember the first time it happened when we were kids.

Grace, Mabel, and I were in the yard jumping rope. Grace was jumping, like she always was because she was the oldest, and Mabel and I were turning the rope with precision. Grace got her foot tangled in the rope and fell to the ground. When we looked up to see what was going on, Mabel was just standing there, staring off into space. She wasn't turning the rope anymore or laughing at Grace's lack of coordination. Instead, she looked like a zombie. Her eyes were frozen forward and her body was completely still. I thought she was dead, but soon realized that if she were, she would surely fall over eventually, and besides, her chest was rising up and down, taking in air. She was breathing, so she must be alive.

Mama and Daddy took her to the doctor after it had happened a few times. They didn't bother to explain the situation to us—instead, we were just instructed to let them know when it happened and make sure she never hurt herself.

The same thing happened throughout the years whenever Mabel got overwhelmed about something. And it wasn't most things that you would think would overwhelm a high school student. It was crazy stuff, like finding the peanut butter jar empty and still sitting in the pantry as if it were filled with the tasty treat. And one time it happened when one of the boys at school asked her to be his girlfriend. I think the kids were just playing, but to Mabel it was real, and no sooner had he gotten the words out of his mouth than she went blank. The kids teased her and I found myself wondering about her time and time again.

There was nothing I could do to help her, but this time it concerned me. The car accident was one of those things that a stable person would have problems handling, and Mabel was far from stable, so what would we do?

"She's gonna be fine, Bev, she's in the best hands she could be in right now. They have the drugs she needs to help her get through this. We just need to make sure we are still there for her after the hospital's cure wears off," Grace said.

Even though I knew Grace wasn't throwing stones at me, I was defensive anyway.

"I've been there for Mabel through the years. Who do you think helped her get that place she's living in now? And we talked at least once a month," I threw back at her.

"I know you did, Bev. I'm not saying any of us neglected Mabel. I'm just saying we need to keep our eye on her after the medication wears off and she has to be strong for Trey."

Grace was being civil; I realized her guard was down, so I put mine down too.

"You know it's right what Mabel said at da house. Dat girl ain' got good sense half da time, but she sho hit it on de money tonight. Da saddest thang is dat we ain' friends no mo," Bobby preached.

We all nodded our heads to acknowledge Bobby's observation. Andrew dialed a number on his cell phone and stepped out onto the balcony for some privacy. I figured he was calling his girlfriend to let her know what was going on. Bobby went into one of the bedrooms and I imagine he was doing the same, but Grace just sat there and stared at me. It wasn't the look like she had given me earlier at her house. It was a look of confusion.

"Where did we go wrong? What did we miss? I'm forty-three years old and I can't for the life of me figure out what happened to this family. One day we were all kids growing up so poor we barely had a pot to pee in. And then we finally got a pot to pee in and lost our damn minds. When we were kids we worked together and stuck together when times were tight and ate the good of the land when times were good. Even as adults we helped Mama and Daddy with the house and even helped with Andrew when they got too sick to take care of him. But now, look at us. What happened, Bev? Well, maybe it's too late to figure that out. What I should be asking is how we get it right?"

I wasn't sure what to say to Grace since I was so caught up in my own grief. Didn't that ole windbag know I had just lost my son, and my daughter was in the hospital? All she wanted to know is what happened to a bunch of adults who are better off living their own lives anyway.

"Bev, do you hear me?"

"I hear you, girl, but my mind is a million miles away. I just lost my son and my husband isn't here yet, and all you can think about is some damn brother-sister mess."

"See, that's part of your problem. You cut off your nose to spite your face. I know you lost your baby and I want to bear the burden with you, but we can't do it under pretenses. We gonna just have to be real, and deal with first things first."

"Be real? Be real? Is that what you want—real!?"

By now, Andrew and Bobby had both come back into the room prepared to break up another tussling match.

"I'll give you real. What do you think it was like all those years, growing up in your shadow? You were always the tall, skinny, pretty one. You could dress nice and frilly and cook a 'mean mess of collards' before you could even see over the stove good. Mama always talked about how you were sure to get a good man and have a lot of good-smelling babies. Well, I got tired of hearing how great Grace was and how wonderful Grace did everything, so I made it my mission to exceed anything you ever accomplished. I would get a better man and have better-smelling babies. Since I couldn't cook, I started writing and took classes to get better at it. I was determined to make it bigger than my big sister Grace. How's that for reality? I use a pen name because all my life Beverly Tayloe wasn't good enough, so I made another Beverly and she's damn good. I have ten best-sellers to my credit and more money than you could ever shake a stick at. So there you have it, Miss Thang, is that real enough?"

Before I could get myself together and suck up the tears, Grace grabbed me and hugged me tight like Mama used to when we were little. She squeezed until I had to let the tears go, or burst. I think I did both. All my life I had resented my sister and spent my days in one-way competition with her. As Grace held me, all the feelings of not measuring up, of being different from Grace because she was tall and slender and a good cook . . . all the old feelings came rushing to the surface of my heart and ran freely down my cheeks in the form of salty forgiveness. I forgave Grace, I forgave Mama, and I forgave myself. In a matter of moments, on this hot July night on the outskirts of Vicksburg, Mississippi, so much had been taken away. Lisa, Junior, and my writing career had been my slap in the face to Grace since she didn't have children and seemed too satisfied working at that stupid national park. I had finally beat her. But I realized I had only beaten myself. I held on to Grace, needing to feel the loving arms of my husband, my children, my parents . . . needing love. And Grace gave it, without ever speaking a word.

My denial and anger were now taking on a new ugly face. I found myself willing to do anything to get my life back. As Grace held on to me, I rocked back and forth, wanting desperately to get one more chance. All I wanted was one chance to make it right. All of it. The rift I created with my siblings, the distance between Michael and I, and the accident. Most importantly, I wanted the minutes back before Lisa, Junior and Trey got into that truck. I begged and pleaded out loud and then quietly to myself. Andrew and Bobby shuffled nervously around from room to room like men do when women are going through emotional stuff. Grace just sat there letting me get it out, watching me beg. Who did I think would hear me? Who would give me that one chance? No one, I realized as the tears went from a downpour to a trickle. No one could bring Junior back, no one could erase the past. The only thing any of us could do anything about was the minutes, hours, and days that lay ahead.

Chapter 16

Michael talked the police escort into taking him to the accident site and hospital first so he was still not at the inn. Bobby and Andrew were sipping coffee while Grace and I talked about the events from earlier in the night: the food, the kids leaving, the police coming to the house. It seemed like a movie replaying in my mind, a real bad movie.

"You know, Mabel gon really need some help afta dis thang set in on her. What y'all thank we need to do? She gon have a hard time lookin' afta Trey," Bobby said.

No one answered immediately. I couldn't bring myself to say a word. It still felt like a nightmare I would certainly wake up from, if I was fortunate enough to find sleep. I wished Michael had come straight to the inn. I was starting to get weak and I needed to see his face for reassurance—assurance that everything would be all right. Who was I kidding? Everything would never be all right.

"Bev, I didn't mean to leave you out, I jus know Mabel by haself and dis gon be hard on her afta, dat's all. It's a bitch bein' by yoself in a situation, specially a real hard situation."

"What do you mean, Bobby? We have always been there for you. At least we've tried to," Andrew added, full well knowing he wasn't including me in the "we all," since I hadn't said more than two words to Bobby in the last eight years.

"When they said you held up that liquor store, Grace and I helped you get bail and everything. What hard situation have you been in without anyone?" Andrew questioned.

"My whole life, man, my whole life. It's all been a bitch. See I was da only boy in da family for so long, and dese girls didn't make it easy on me. Grace was always in Mama and Daddy's face wit some new project she was workin' on. She was either cookin' wit Mama or redecoratin' de house while Daddy ranted and raved 'bout dat. And Bev, she jus kept takin' dem classes at da Y and gettin' dose writin' awards. All through school dey were doin' dis or dat and it jus overshadowed a brother."

"So it was our fault that you couldn't seem to find your way," Grace added coldly.

Her tone shocked me, considering the fact that it was 4:00 in the morning and Bobby seemed to be trying to reach out to us. Even I could see that, and I always chose to see the worst in Bobby.

"Dat's right, Grace, 'cause whether you noticed or not, I was da one workin' odd jobs to help pay fo some of dat stuff y'all was doin'. I worked here and there to make money so Bev could take dem classes and buy all dem damn notebooks. By da way, what you do wit all dem notebooks anyway?"

I was shocked by Bobby's question and I almost didn't have an answer since it had been years since I looked through any of my old notebooks from early writing projects.

"I guess they're somewhere in the attic in Melrose. I'm not sure."

"Anyway, I started trying to do somethin' so I could get some of dat attention too. I didn't have no special talent, so I jus used my head to find work so I could help pay for y'all. Daddy and Mama seemed appreciative, but it still wasn't da same as actually doin' somethin' myself. So dat's when I tried to go to college. I never wanted to go to college. I knew da first day I walked into dat place dat I didn't belong. I wanted out so bad, I didn't know what to do. I kept goin' 'cause dat's what y'all did, and dat had to be da right thang to do. Everybody was still singing da praises of Grace and Bev. Mama and Daddy was jus happy Mabel could hold down a job and help take care of herself, but I knew dey expected mo from me. Strong black man spose to be 'bout mo," he went on with a distant look in his eyes.

"When college wasn't workin' out, I jus did da thang dat seemed most natural—da women." He got a smile out of Andrew from two men understanding one another.

"Dem crazy-ass women made me think I was God's gift to dis world until dey dumb-asses started gettin' pregnant on me, so dey could git dey check. Everything went downhill after dat. Dropped out of college and became da project-ho sperm bank. Now, you see dat don't really measure up either, but dat's what happened."

"So, Bobby, if you didn't want to go to college, what did you want to do?" I asked with the most compassion I could muster the morning after such a trying night.

"I jus wanted to work at da cemetery like Daddy. He always seemed to enjoy it, and it looked like honorable work, but after I got a criminal record, dat was out of da question. Dey wouldn't hire me even if I said I would work fo free."

"Why did you get into trouble that time? If you were always working and trying to do good, why did you get caught stealing?" Grace offered, again showing no love for her oldest brother.

"Grace, I wasn't stealin', I was borrowin' it. I had all intentions of puttin' da money back."

We all laughed at that one—all of us except Bobby.

"I was sixteen years old and Bev had written home 'bout some money she needed. You member, Bev, it was fo dat thang you wrote dat won da award. Well, somebody wanted to publish it and you needed money fo somethin'. I was on da other line listenin' when Daddy told you he didn't have da money and you needed to jus stick wit yo schoolwork and stop tryin' to be all high and mighty like you some kinda writer or somethin'."

I remembered the conversation so well, I could almost hear Daddy's words as Bobby talked. I had won an essay contest at school and needed extra money to attend the next phase of the contest. The winner of the national award would be published in *Newsweek*. It would be my first published work, but again money was the issue. I hated calling home for money because I knew with Mama and Daddy trying to take care of three kids and pay my way through college, it was a tough time.

"Well, I took dat money out of Mr. Jernigan's cash register to send it to you 'cause my paycheck wasn't quite enough. I was gonna put it back when I got paid da next time, but I was so nervous, I got caught. Mr. Jernigan tipped right up behine me and dere I was standin' dere wit da money in my hand like one guilty nigger. He called da police so quick it made my head spin."

Bobby kept talking about the experience like it was some scene out of a bad John Wayne movie, but all I could think about was the fact that my brother was trying to look out for me. He was even willing to steal to help me. He, at sixteen, saw how important it was for me to get into that competition. I remembered Andrew's words at the grave site earlier. Bobby had gotten some bad breaks, and part of the problem was caring about his family too much.

"Bev, I don mean to be so hard on you and your uppity-behind husband. I jus hate dat you don let folk know who you really are. I like your writing. I mean da stuff you usta write befo you were rich and famous. I like da stuff you write now; I jus don understand all of it. But I'm proud of you and all I wanted to do was be a part of what you was doin' since I couldn't seem to do nuthin' myself. Dat's all," Bobby finished.

I couldn't speak. Bobby sat across the room with his head hung low like a child who had been scolded one time too many. I looked at Andrew and then Grace. They were both waiting for something, either Bobby to start talking again or me to say something. They waited. I did too.

"Bev, I'm sorry 'bout yo children. We need to take dat money they gone give us from dat land, and do somethin' to help Lisa and Trey and some other kids, too. Somebody like you was when you needed to pay fo dat competition."

"You mean like a scholarship fund?" I asked, talking to Bobby for the first time ever as if he was an intelligent human being and not my slack-ass younger brother.

"Yeah, a scholarship fo kids already in college doin' somethin' fo themselves, but jus need some extra money to help pay for stuff like dat competition or other stuff dat come up dat could make a difference in their careers."

"Bobby, I think you got it. A scholarship fund," I responded, but before I could finish, Grace chimed in with the specifics.

While Grace was talking, I thought about how ridiculous it was to be sitting here planning a way to help other kids when my son was gone. I wanted to get angry again at the insensitivity of my brothers and sister, but I kept quiet.

"The Bobby Lavon Tayloe Scholarship in memory of Michael Lamark, Jr. Name it after Bobby since he always had enough sense to try to help us, even when we didn't know he was trying to help. It should be enough money to give some to several students each year in thousand-dollar increments. As Tayloe offspring we could continue to add to the fund as we get extra money. I'll start tonight with an additional thousand dollars I just got as a bonus from work," Grace said.

"I'll add an additional thousand too," Andrew added.

There they were, throwing in money to help some kids we didn't even know. How the hell was that supposed to make me feel better? I didn't give a damn about some other kids needing scholarship money, I just wanted my son back. If that money was gonna do anything, it would help my Junior do something.

There it was again. Every time I tried to maintain a stream of rational thought, it happened: the reality of death slapped me in the face. There was nothing Junior would ever do with any money. He was gone. As much as I tried to concentrate on Lisa and her well-being, my mind kept drifting back to my loss. I left the room on that note, realizing I was not on the same page with everyone else.

When Andrew followed me, part of me wanted to cuss him out and blame it on grief and the other wanted to talk and let someone feel what I was feeling. They obviously didn't, to just sit there and talk about handing out money like Junior had never even existed.

"Bev, did we say something wrong out there?" Andrew asked, as he shut the door behind him.

"Well, not really, but I'm just not in the mood to divvy up money when I still can't come to terms with the fact that my baby is gone."

"I'm sorry, Bev, we just weren't thinking. We can just talk about that stuff later. Michael will be here soon and you all need to start notifying people about . . ."

"Go ahead, say it. Say it, say his name—Junior—don't you dare not say his name. Don't avoid his name. Say his name, dammit; I need to hear you say it. I can't let him slip away from me and just hearing his name keeps him here for me."

I couldn't blame Andrew. I had done it plenty of times myself—avoid people who had just lost a loved one because I didn't know what to say. Especially someone who had lost a baby or child. Who wants to be around that awkward situation? What can you say? I never knew until this moment. The last thing you do is avoid their names. That's their own individual link to the fact that their child was a part of this world.

Michael Lamark, Jr., part of a scholarship fund. My heart accepted it. The scholarship fund was my family's way of saying his name, not just once, but as long as the fund existed. As long as the fund existed, Junior would be with us.

As my temper tantrum changed over to a personal revelation, Andrew twirled his hands one over the other as if waiting for me to rejoin the sane. I almost giggled as I watched him trying to avoid whatever stage of grief I was pulsating through. After I gave him that you're-off-the-hook look, we joined the others and, of course, I added a thousand each for myself and Mabel. Bobby said he could probably come up with the money, if he had the green-eyed baby tested for paternity, but that baby needed to eat too, so he couldn't spare anything right now. He was already running a charity, so I tossed in his share.

There we sat working on a scholarship fund for other kids. It didn't make sense and when Michael walked in, I was too embarrassed to admit what we had been doing. But the Tayloe brothers and sisters understood it all. It's who we are; it's how we were raised. No outsider, even my husband, could be part of what we did that night in the Cedar Grove Inn Centennial Suite. Grace, Beverly, Bobby, and Andrew Tayloe fought back. With our backs against the wall and our hearts in our hands, we found the true spirit of what our parents were all about, and we each found ourselves, and we silently vowed to keep the next generation alive the best way we could.

When Michael walked through the door, he had a troubling look on his face. There was a police officer with him, and after they exchanged a few words, Michael came into the suite to join us, and the officer went on his way. I wasn't sure if I should approach him, or keep my distance and let him come to me. He looked like he wasn't sure what to feel.

"Hi, Michael. We're sorry, man," Andrew offered as Michael took a seat on the sofa. We had all been so wrapped up in our discussion and our own thoughts that we weren't sure what to say to Michael. Grace and Bobby all offered their condolences and gave Michael a hug. And then it was my turn.

"Hi, baby. We can go into one of the bedrooms for privacy if you want."

He didn't respond. He just looked around the room, rubbed his hand over the top of his head like he was in deep thought, and then he got up. He walked toward the kitchen area, where everyone had moved to give us some space. He looked at them all, but still said nothing. He looked toward one of the bedrooms, and then just started walking toward it like a zombie. I followed, not sure what else to do.

"Michael, honey, did you go to the hospital? Did you get to see Lisa?"

He finally spoke, using a cold, harsh tone I'd never heard from my husband of seventeen years.

"Of course I went to the hospital. Yes, I saw Lisa and then they took me to the morgue and I saw, but I still can't believe it."

He dropped his head between his legs. I wasn't sure if he was crying or trying to get himself together. I waited.

"Bev, how did this happen?"

I wasn't sure how to respond to his tone. His words were simple enough, but the tone was much more complex. I kept my distance, feeling more like his enemy than his wife. I leaned against a dresser in the room. I sighed and tried to find the words that would meet his tone properly. He didn't give me a chance.

"Bev, the officer said Lisa and Trey had alcohol in their systems. Where could they have gotten alcohol? And why were they out so late, by themselves? We never let Lisa drive at that time of night at home. What the hell were you thinking?"

Michael was looking for someone to blame and I was the likely candidate. I didn't feel I had a leg to stand on in my defense. The night before, we were robbed and all because of my negligence. I knew Michael thought the worst about this situation too. And the bad part was that this time I couldn't reassure him that everything was fine, because our son was gone.

"Bev, say something, dammit, don't just stand there. I need answers. How could this happen? There were at least five adults around—how did three teenagers get alcohol and then get behind the wheel of an automobile? How, Bev?"

"Michael, first of all you need to watch your damn tone with me. I have been through hell just like you and they are my kids too. You can make all the accusations you want, but you weren't there."

"You're right, I wasn't there, so tell me what the hell happened. You were there, weren't you?"

"Look, I can't talk to you when you're like this. I am hurting just like you, and regardless of what happened, you can't bring him back by taking it out on me."

"Okay, so tell me who I can blame. Who's responsible?"

I couldn't deal with the interrogation, so I stormed out of the room, sobbing loud enough to get everyone else's attention. I had forgotten they were there, so I kept walking right out the door and into the parking lot. The police car was still there. The innkeeper light was on in the main house. I wanted to think about what they might be doing in the middle of the night with the innkeeper, but I had my own irrational husband to deal with. No sooner had I gotten to the edge of the front porch of the inn than Michael walked up behind me, grabbed me, and spun me around with too much force.

"Listen, dammit. You can't run away from this. I need answers. My son is dead and I damn well better hear your version of what happened."

"I cannot believe you are trying to make me feel like this is my fault. Even if you feel that way, Michael, that just isn't fair. I've been through too much to blame myself for this, and to think that you want to make me out as the culprit is more than I can handle."

"So you'll just run off and leave me hanging. You have a real habit of running off when things make you uncomfortable, Bev. But not this time. You ran from your damn family for years, but I will not let you run off and not give me some answers."

"Michael . . ."

The officer interrupted what was about to be a desperate plea to get Michael off my back. He asked us to step inside the inn; he had information on the accident.

"Mr. and Mrs. Lamark, I'm Officer Telfair and I'm investigating what happened last night. As you already know, alcohol was found in the kid's bloodstream. We believe it may have had something to do with the accident, but we aren't sure. The accident could have been the result of teenagers being teenagers and not paying full attention to driving."

"Not my Lisa, she was a good driver—I taught her myself. She wouldn't let anything distract her. She knew better than to fiddle with the radio or cell phone or anything like that when driving," Michael said.

"Yes, sir, well, sir, that's all the more reason we need to find out about the alcohol. Do you all have any idea how they might have obtained alcohol?"

Michael and the officer looked at me. I was under the gun this time. The whole scene with Michael and now this conversation with the officer was adding up to too much stress. I couldn't feel anything anymore.

"I think they got the alcohol and came back here to the inn and drank it because I found a beer bottle cap inside the suite."

"Ma'am, do you know where they might have gotten the alcohol?"

"I—they were going to a store near my sister Grace's house, but I'm not sure which store. Maybe they got it there."

I glanced at Michael. He was not getting satisfaction from my answers. Why didn't I know where the kids had gone? What kind of parent wouldn't keep better track of her fourteen- and sixteen-year-old in a strange city?

"Mrs. Lamark, we'll try to get the name of the store from your sister. We would like to give your daughter and nephew more time before we get into this with them."

That was a good idea since Grace knew every nook and cranny on her side of town. She'd certainly know what store Trey was planning to take them to. I nodded my head yes.

"Ma'am, I hate to belabor the point, but could they have gotten the alcohol from anywhere else? Did you have alcohol in your suite, or at your sister's house?"

"No, sir, I know Grace didn't have any alcohol—she forbids it in her house. I didn't have any in the suite, although I had a couple of drinks early this afternoon before going to Grace's. But I drank them right here in the inn, at the bar."

"Were they with you when you ordered the drinks?"

I knew where he was going with his questions. I'd heard of parents who let their children experiment. I couldn't let him think that about me.

"No, of course not, Lisa knows I wouldn't let her drink. She would never get alcohol behind my back like . . ."

I paused, realizing I was contradicting myself. She *had* gotten alcohol behind my back. I wasn't sure what to think and Michael was no help. He wasn't offering one single ounce of support, only condemnation and judgment.

"So, Bev, did the kids see you get drinks at the bar? What did you drink? Did you get beers?" Michael asked.

"No, Michael, I don't even drink beer, I got—I got a couple of mint juleps."

"Mint juleps? When the hell did you start drinking mint juleps?"

"Michael, you don't know every damn thing I do."

"Apparently not. What else are you gonna surprise me with, Bev?"

"Excuse me, I think maybe we should go with what we have so far and try to find out what store the kids went to near your sister's house. Where is your sister?"

I pointed the officer toward the suite at the back of the property. I glanced at Michael again, and I could almost see steam coming out of his ears. He was not pleased with where this was heading. He definitely blamed me.

"Mrs. Lamark—Mrs. Lamark, over here," the innkeeper motioned from the front door of the main house. "We need to talk with you. Please come inside."

I walked toward the house with Michael at my side. I had no idea what they were going to hit me with now, but if it was anything like what had already happened, it wouldn't be good.

"Mrs. Lamark, the officer told us what happened. We decided to ask our staff if they saw anything tonight, if they saw the kids here at the inn."

"Well, I know they were here. We found a beer cap on the floor in the suite, so we know they came here to drink."

"Mrs. Lamark, this is Hal, he's the bartender that was on duty tonight."

I remembered the tall slim man who looked barely old enough to drink himself. He had served me when I got my drinks earlier that afternoon.

"Mrs. Lamark, I got a call from your suite tonight, um, probably around eight-thirty, and you ordered a couple of juleps and a six-pack. I started to question the call for so much alcohol, but it's not our practice to question what customers do in the privacy of their suite. I just figured you had . . . you know . . . company. You told me that you were going to send your son over to get the things because you had already gotten ready for bed. I remembered you from the bar earlier, and I remembered you ordered the julep, so I didn't question the order any further. I got the drinks ready and when your son came in to get the stuff, he paid using your credit card, and, well, ma'am, I was just sure everything was on the level. We were kind of busy and, well . . ."

Hal was clearly feeling caught in the middle of the situation. He had filled an order he thought was placed by me, and he didn't question it because he was trying to be accommodating to the guest. It made sense to me, but Michael's look was saying something else altogether.

"Do you usually give mixed drinks and six-packs to fourteen-year-old kids? Didn't you think to question the situation at all?"

"Sir, I did question it a little, because I thought Mrs. Lamark was here with just the kids, but then I assumed she had company, or maybe she just wanted to tie one on. I'm a bartender. I'm accustomed to people drinking a good amount of alcohol. And ma'am, it sounded just like you on the phone; she ordered the drinks just like you had earlier and . . . I just didn't . . ."

By now Michael had thrown up his hands in disgust and walked out the front door. No sooner had he got out the door than the officer was coming back in. We told him about the drink order and Hal pulled the copy of my credit card receipt and made a copy for the officer. I left the officer and Hal in the front lobby, going over the details. I needed to find Michael, even though he was the last person in the world I wanted to see. Everything was happening much too fast. My head was hurting and for the life of me, I couldn't figure out why the hell Lisa had done something so stupid. I didn't want to think about what had really happened. I wanted to know my kids were smarter than that, but the harsh reality was setting in and the new sun was coming up over the horizon. I finally spotted Michael standing near one of the gardens toward the back of the inn's main house. I wanted to just leave him alone with his negative-ass attitude, but I knew the longer I let him go, the tougher it would be for us to come to terms with what had happened.

"Michael, let's talk about it."

"Bev, I just can't get my mind to accept that he's gone and Lisa and Trey are in the hospital. Something just isn't clicking in my head."

He broke down and let the tears flow. I could see the anger and rage mixed with grief and despair as it rolled down his cheeks and splashed in a small puddle on the damp soil below. I didn't speak. There was nothing to say. He knew what had happened—not all the details, but enough. Enough to finally start processing the ugly truth. I sat down by his side because I was supposed to. I couldn't cry. I was numb. The sun was still rising. The horrible night was stretching into another day as I sat beside Michael and watched his soul groan and lament.

In the distance, I saw Bobby and Andrew coming out of the suite.

I left Michael briefly to fill them in on what we had learned in those early morning hours. They both hugged me as they headed out to get ready to meet with the EDC. I had forgotten about that part. The sun was casting a stream of red and orange hues across the inn landscape and I realized life had to go on. Business as usual. Bobby and Andrew drove off and Grace soon followed. She was headed to the hospital to check on Mabel and Trey.

I returned to Michael's side. His tears had tapered off slightly and he was ready to talk. I was still numb.

"So, what now?" he asked. "I've never done this before. I guess we need to call people and let the family know what happened. And we need to make . . . arrangements."

He broke down again. This time I put my arm around him as he leaned on my shoulder and let the pain continue to stream from his now-swollen eyes. In the distance, the officer was leaving, Hal was getting into his car, and the innkeepers were standing on the porch holding large coffee cups. The wife held up her cup, motioning to me that they were for us. I nodded my head as they started to head toward their grief-stricken guests.

"Thought you might need a cup of Joe, as you Northerners call it," the innkeeper said with a lighthearted humor that lifted some of the fog Michael and I were engulfed in.

"Thank you," we both said as we took the coffee and started sipping the life source.

"We'll help you out with whatever we can. You can have that suite as long as you need it, our treat," he graciously added.

"We appreciate that."

"There's a section of the inn that we usually shut down for a couple of weeks for heavy-duty cleaning. We can open that up if you need room for out-of-town family."

They were being so accommodating. They had gotten caught up in the middle of our tragedy and they were doing what any decent Southern person would do.

"Thank you again. We'll keep that in mind as we make... arrangements." I, too, stumbled on the words just as Michael had earlier. We were making funeral arrangements for our son. I let the idea settle in my mind as the innkeepers went back to the main house.

Michael and I agreed to go ahead and have the services in Mississippi instead of trying to move things back to Massachusetts. We didn't have family up there anyway, and Michael's immediate family could fly in from New York. So, we prepared ourselves for whatever the first step was in making arrangements.

I went into the suite to grab a shower while Michael made calls. I overheard him periodically struggling to tell family, friends, and coworkers about the unfortunate events. I dressed, not having any idea what you wear for such a day. It really didn't matter. Nothing we were doing felt right: telling people our son was dead, contacting the mortician's office and setting up an appointment, getting the autopsy report from the hospital.

After we had called everyone, Michael and I flopped down, trying to brace ourselves for the toughest day we'd ever faced.

"Michael, we can get through this if we stick together. I have to know you don't blame me."

"Bev, I'm just hurting. Of course I don't blame you, I'm just confused and hurt, and my chest is aching like I'm having a heart attack or something. I keep hoping someone will wake me up from this nightmare and you and Lisa and Junior will drive up in the truck, and we'll all hug and everything will be all right."

We tried to make an action plan. We needed to do things in a logical order. Hospital first, to check on Lisa and Trey, then the mortician. I let Michael know where Grace, Bobby, and Andrew had gone. Everyone was working together and getting the necessary things taken care of. As alone as we felt, we weren't. I had brothers and sisters out there taking care of things I had neither the strength nor patience to deal with.

"So I guess you guys dealt with your issues and decided what to do with the land," Michael finally said, unaware of the night's events before he had arrived.

I nodded my head as Michael breathed an almost silent "Amen."

We sat there a moment or two longer, trying to get our feet to move us in the direction of making arrangements. As we walked out of the inn and got into the car Michael had rented at the airport, I couldn't help but think of his accusations. Michael was all about being practical. He never did irrational things and he would never have let the kids go anyplace without asking a million questions and giving a lecture. He would have found out which store they were going to and how long it should take them to get there and back. He would have looked at his watch when they drove off and if they had been even minutes late, he would have been on the road looking for them. My actions never made sense to him—they never had—and I was convinced that after this, they never would. To him, his way was always right, not just different from mine. As we drove along the now-busy streets of downtown Vicksburg, I knew he blamed me and always would.

Chapter 17

Lisa was doing better by the time we got to the hospital. Michael and I had agreed to keep the conversation to a minimum and not mention the alcohol. I watched as Michael leaned in to hear her and give her a kiss. Her tears ran and so did his, but they comforted each other. I watched like an outsider. Michael was giving Lisa reassurance, a good thing to get when you feel responsible for a tragedy. I looked away from the two of them, jealous for what he was giving her so freely. I looked at the thick dust on the blinds, wondering how long it had been since anyone had run a cloth over them. I wanted to think of anything except the fact that I was the bad guy. And I had no one to lean on.

I remembered Daddy saying a long time ago that we children wouldn't complain so much if we had to walk a mile in his shoes. Today, walking two steps seemed like the most difficult thing I had ever done. We let Lisa know that Aunt Grace would be picking her up at noon. She was okay with that and didn't bother to ask questions about where Michael and I were headed. She already knew. We peeked in on Trey, but he was finally resting, so we quietly left without saying a word.

With the hospital deals behind us, all we had to do was go to the funeral home and work on the details with the mortician. I say, all we had to do, as if that wasn't a huge thing to have to take on—talking to a mortician about a funeral for your fourteen-year-old child. I wouldn't wish that feeling on my worst enemy.

Andrew and Bobby were meeting with the EDC people at 9:00 AM and then going to the bank to set up some kind of account, so we would have a place to deposit and disperse the money from the sale. The EDC people were already counting on us selling the land, so they had an attorney on standby to handle the transaction. We had all planned to be sitting there with the EDC people, but Mabel, Grace and I had other things to attend to. We were confident that the men of the family would handle that part, and by nightfall we would all get together again to discuss the arrangements for the sale of the land and the funeral.

Michael and I got to the funeral home at 9:00 AM. The mortician met us in the front lobby of the old, run-down building that could easily have doubled as a juke joint. As soon as we stepped inside, there it was—that awful funeral music. Who the hell wants to hear funeral music at 9:00 in the morning? I think it was the same song they were playing when Daddy died—sad-ass funeral music, as if you need anything else to bring you down.

After the mortician spouted off some words at Michael, we met with the person handling the finances. She was a slender, tall woman who reminded me of Grace in her better days. This woman was easily in her late forties but didn't look a day over thirty-five. I hated her on sight. She was polite and articulate and surely sleeping with Mr. Mortician guy. I picked that up from the glances shooting back and forth between them. They were probably going at it before we walked in. I heard those mortician people are kind of freaky. I guess you have to be when you work with dead bodies all day.

Michael was shaking his head up and down, so I thought I'd better pay attention and stop thinking about the kinky sex lives of funeral home people. It's amazing the crazy things that pop into your mind when you're sleep-deprived and grieving. You'd have thought

I'd be concentrating on the sad truth before me, but instead all I could do was wonder if he had been doing her on that desk when we drove up.

My mind drifted in and out during the entire meeting with the mortician and the money lady. Michael was handling everything anyway. They attributed my lack of response to my grief and loss, and not my silly imagination running wild, avoiding the grief and loss. I didn't want to think about the casket, and the burial plan, and all that stuff. I wanted to get into my truck, with my children, and head back home like I had planned. None of this was supposed to happen.

Grace was right beside us at the mortician's. She had been handling things for Mabel, who was still drugged up and likely to stay that way. Bobby was right—we'd have to figure out what to do for Mabel when this was all over. There I was again, thinking of anything except what I was in this godforsaken place to do: funeralize my baby. Grace sat beside Michael, nodding her head. It's like she knew I was off in my own world. She had come to offer support.

Andrew called from his cell phone and let us know that he and Bobby had wrapped up things with the EDC and were headed over to the bank now. They had the check—$75,000—in hand and would deposit it in Andrew's name since he had connections at the bank and could do it without a whole lot of red tape. We would set up the scholarship fund and all that later. For now, we had the money, and that part was behind us. After the funeral arrangements were completed, Michael and I went to Grace's church with her to meet with her pastor to ask about having the funerals there. I think I was dreading the whole church scene more than I had dreaded the funeral home. At least at the funeral home, you know it's all about death. At church, it's supposed to be about life and joy and peace, but it's usually about death too.

The pastor was a different guy from the one who was there when Daddy died. These pastors didn't stick around as long as they did back in the day. I think the one that was there when Daddy died moved to a larger church, and then the one after him got caught messing around some skirt tails he should have stayed away from. They ran him out of town so fast, the ink hadn't dried on his business cards. (I made that part up, but it sounded good anyway.) This guy seemed nice enough. He was short and stocky, the kind of guy you'd imagine sounded kind of wimpy on the pulpit. He shook Michael's hand and then mine and we proceeded into his office. The office was laid out; the Pastor's Aid Club must have been on the job this time—nice cherry oak furniture with a bookcase full of religious writings, most of which I had never even heard of. Either he was well read or knew how to fake it real good. He sat down behind his huge desk and stared solemnly at Michael and I before opening his mouth.

"Our current policy usually prevents us from eulogizing non-members, but we are gonna make an exception in this case, and all we need to know is the name of your current pastor and the church where you pay your tithe," he finished in that wimpy tone that made me want to reach behind that desk and slap his face.

I wanted to jump right up then and there and storm out of this den of thieves, when Grace took over the conversation. I could tell from her first words that she ran things around here. Ole pastor was just a figurehead and the ladies of the church still made the calls. Some things never changed. That was comforting. At least I knew the Pillsbury Doughboy wouldn't be running the show for my son's funeral.

The words stuck in my head for the first time. This wasn't a birthday party or get-together at the house—I was planning a funeral for my son. I needed a stiff drink and was just about to ask Rev. Shorty for a shot of that fifth he likely kept in his desk, but I didn't want to further aggravate Grace. I kept my crazy thoughts to myself and listened as Grace and Michael now talked about the service and who would do what.

The reverend still didn't sound like he wanted to let us have he services there since we couldn't give him the name of our pastor and church where we pay our tithe. What the hell did that have to do with wanting to have the funeral there? I thought that's what churches were for—helping the hurting and reaching out to the community and people like Michael and me who didn't see the need for church. If this was our opportunity to come to Jesus, Rev. Shorty would not be scoring the home run for the Lord. I had been out of the flow so long, I guess it had all changed. This hotbed of political activists and financial prosperity was the last place I wanted to spend my last moments with my son, but I kept that to myself too, and let Grace have her way with the reverend.

We left St. Thomas, church of the short and stocky, just after lunchtime and by then my head was throbbing and I knew it was lack of sleep, caffeine, and food. I was on my way to get at least two of the three. Michael stopped at a tiny café near the church. He called Andrew and we all agreed to meet back at the inn. We would have gone back to Grace's, but she had moved Mabel and Lisa there so they could get some rest. I think Grace went ahead and moved Mabel there because she knew in her heart of hearts that Mabel wasn't going to bounce back from this one, and Grace's house would likely be her permanent residence.

When we got to the inn, Michael went inside to meet with the guys and go over the details of their meeting with the EDC. I wasn't ready for business talk, or much else, so I wandered toward the garden near the back of the property, the one with the view of the river. There was a small bench there so I sat, not knowing what else to do. The mortician and church people were all handling the next phases and within a matter of hours we would be in the middle of the worst thing that could ever happen to a parent: burying a child.

"I don't want to bother you. I saw you sitting here and I just wanted to offer my condolences. I heard."

It was Victor. He had genuine concern on his face and a cup of tea in his hand. I needed both. I motioned for him to join me on the bench. I had learned one thing the night before with my brothers and sisters: when you come to a certain point in life, you have to be honest, be real, before you can move on.

"Thank you. I guess everyone knows by now."

"The innkeepers let us all know since there were questions about the police cars last night."

"Oh, yeah. That almost seems like days ago, not hours."

"Is there anything I can do?"

"This is good—tea and a shoulder to lean on."

"I think I can handle that. Is your husband here?"

"Yes, and, well, let's just say it's going to be tough to get past this one."

He looked off into the distance toward the river. He smelled nice. I hated myself more for wanting him near, for needing him to be sitting with me during such a personal time.

"If you look down that way, the river almost looks like it goes on forever."

I looked downriver as Victor slipped his hand into mine. I sipped the tea, trying to ignore the feeling. It had been so long. It wasn't an inappropriate touch, but the kind of unconditional support a woman longs for—no blame, no slanted insinuations, just support. I leaned on it, and allowed myself to depend on it. And, for a brief moment, time stood still as Old Man River gave me a glimpse of how love would eventually wash over the pain in my heart, ripple by ripple.

I don't remember when Victor left. I still felt his hand in mine even though he was long gone. I knew I would feel it for some time to come. I left the garden as dusk settled on the flowers and greenery that made this one of the most beautiful places on the face of the earth. The five acres of gardens that surrounded the inn consisted of everything including an Italian gazebo that led to a brick walkway with rose-covered arbors. There were a few hammocks on the property where you could lie back and be lulled to sleep by water trickling from a fountain or the swaying of a graceful crepe myrtle.

As I sat there thinking about all the things that had gone wrong, I spotted an elderly couple walking from the main house to their car. They were holding hands and sharing a tender moment as if they were two lovers stealing away for a romantic rendezvous. They were at least sixty years old, so I ruled out the rendezvous and settled on the idea that they were just a happily married couple enjoying the fruits of their labor. They had likely been together for years, worked hard, raised children, retired, and now were basking in the wonder of Cedar Grove presence. I imagined a scene from one of the romance novels I'd read over the years, the perfect love story where everything worked out in the end, where lovers faced trouble, endured hardship, and loved stronger and more fervently when it was all said and done. Why didn't it ever happen like that in real life?

When I walked into the suite, the men were talking. I didn't care to join their discussion. Grace was sitting in the kitchen with the look of a woman who needed a friend. I motioned for her to join me in one of the bedrooms.

"Are you okay?" I asked her.

"The question is are you okay? Who was that man?"

"No one."

"That's so far from the truth. I didn't think you knew anyone here. It's been years since you set foot in Vicksburg—how do you know him, and so well?"

"I don't know him. I met him yesterday when I got here. He's no one."

"Yeah, I don't buy that for one minute. Remember, I had my Leroy. I know what it looks like."

I didn't want to talk to Grace about this. I wanted her to think that things were perfect between Michael and me, that we were just like any other couple. We had our tough spots, but we were committed to each other and we would get through this. The last person I wanted to talk to about my loveless marriage was Grace. Although, she was probably the best person to talk to, since she knew true love firsthand.

"Grace, we'll be fine. We will."

"But you haven't been fine, and now this. Solid couples have trouble dealing with tragedy. Do you really believe you'll get through it? What you gonna do, take Mr. Nobody back to Melrose with you for support?"

"What is it, Grace, what are we missing?"

"Where do I begin? You always thought we disliked Michael because of his nationality. I could care less about where he's from and what his customs are. I just knew he didn't make you glow."

"Glow? What the hell . . . who glows?"

"Women in love, men in love."

Grace saw right through my meager attempts to hide my feelings, so I listened.

"You never had any sparkle in your tone when you talked about Michael. You never got giddy when you first told us about him. You didn't act like you had found your soul mate."

"Now, you know I don't believe in that mess."

"Obviously not, since you didn't bother to wait for yours."

"So Leroy was your soul mate?"

She paused. I was afraid I had made a mistake in bringing it up again. The last thing I wanted to do was upset her. She had been so good for me in the few hours since we'd started acting like rational adults.

"It kinda feels like the two of you met someplace before. Like you have always known each other, just didn't meet until, well, whenever you meet. Crazy, but it feels like you were once one person and then somehow got separated. Then out of nowhere you find him again. And you know it on sight. It tingles and flutters, like butterflies in your stomach."

I didn't hear much of the other stuff she said. She scared the daylights out of me when she said tingle. I wanted to run from the conversation. Too much was happening too fast. I didn't need Grace to tell me about soul mates and butterflies. I tuned her out and quickly found a way to get out of that room and join the others for funeral planning. Not that I was ready for that either.

Chapter 18

We sat around the suite and planned the funeral service. Grace assured us that the choir would do at least three or four tasteful selections of uplifting music, none of that make-me-cry funeral music. The good reverend would lead the service, but we did not want him to deliver the eulogy. It didn't seem appropriate—he didn't know my son. Grace did not want the responsibility and Andrew didn't think it was his place to do something so important. After going around and around the issue, I agreed to speak.

After I said it, I wanted to take it back. I would likely be a basket case with a church full of people thinking bad thoughts about the irresponsible adults who were supposed to be looking out for the three teenagers. They had to be thinking that. Many of the people who would be at the funeral had seen Grace and me rolling around her front yard like toddlers. Those who hadn't seen it had likely gotten a play-by-play from gossiping neighbors. Everyone in Vicksburg and neighboring towns would turn out to see the Tayloe family act like complete fools in their grief.

I couldn't change my mind. I had to be the one to speak over Junior. It was settled. Bobby suggested burying him at the cemetery where Mama and Daddy and much of the Tayloe family were laid to rest. Michael objected, mentioning his own family burial plot. He mumbled over and over about how he wanted his kids to be buried in that plot. We all just listened. He finally threw his hands up and said to hell with it and left the suite.

I didn't go after him. I couldn't face the accusations. We settled it, that he would be buried at Brownstone Cemetery. Next, where would the feeding take place? That part bothered me most. Who cares where the feeding takes place? It's just another uncomfortable situation for a grieving family, as if food is on your mind just hours after burying a family member.

"Bev, it's still got to be done," Grace said. "I know it doesn't make sense, but the sisters from church will handle all the food. We just need to decide where to do it. The church dining hall is available to us, but we can always do it at my house."

We all opted for Grace's house and, with that, the feeding was taken care of. Grace put the final touches on the program and left to take it to Sister Marshall who was going to type it up and get the copies made for the service. Grace wanted to keep busy, so this was good for her. I wanted to be busy, just so I would have an excuse not to go out looking for my husband. But no suck luck.

I found him sitting on the inn porch. I was surprised to see him sitting right out in the open like that. He wasn't crying this time. He didn't have that distant look in his eye.

"Want some company?"

He didn't answer. I sat down beside him anyway.

"We don't have to talk if you don't want to. But I don't think the distance is good for us either."

"So what do you suggest, since you seem to be the authority on what we should and shouldn't do?"

"Michael, let's not do this again."

"What are we supposed to do, Bev? I was just arguing with your family about where to bury my son."

He got up and walked off, still mumbling under his breath. I wanted to follow him, but my feet wouldn't move. I didn't have the strength to fight that battle. I had enough to deal with. I couldn't start blaming myself. I couldn't. I had a eulogy to prepare for.

The worst thing that could have happened, did. Victor had overheard my conversation with Michael. He walked up just as Michael left. He was not what I needed right then. He was the last person I needed to see, but the only one there.

"Do you want to talk? We could go to my suite."

On a normal day I would have just let it go, turned him down and gone on my way, but ever since I got Mabel's letter, nothing had been normal. I needed a break from it all. I couldn't go a step further with all this stuff on my shoulders.

When we got to his suite, I uncomfortably looked around, realizing he had the bare necessities and nothing more. His room was nothing like the Centennial. His room was just that: a room with a bathroom and a tiny sitting area in the corner. He had a laptop computer set up on the table and, other than a pair of stonewashed jeans thrown over the back of the chair, the room was tidy. The queen-size bed was made, although I tried not to look at it. It represented a forbidden place I couldn't let my mind venture toward.

"Make yourself comfortable, Bev."

He called me Bev as if we had known each other forever. I sat down on the chair with the jeans on it. He didn't attempt to move them. There were so many emotions tangled up in knots in my stomach, I wasn't sure if I wanted to talk or cry or just sit there leaning back on those stonewashed jeans. So I sat still, looking into space.

"Can I get you something? A Coke, or a cup of decaf?"

"No, Victor, really, I shouldn't even be here. I'm not sure why I am. I just . . . it's too much right now."

I got up to leave, but he stopped me at the door. He stood there in front of me, at least six inches taller than me. He stood closer than he had in the garden the first day, or in my suite when he dropped

167

off the credit card. The short-sleeved button-down white shirt he was wearing had that right-out-of-the-dryer look. Either he didn't know the rooms all came with an iron, or he didn't care. He wore a faded pair of Levi's with a hole at the knee in the left pant leg and a hole just below his right pocket, probably from carrying his keys there. The top two buttons on his shirt were undone and revealed just a hint of chest hair. I forced my eyes to steer clear of that and the hole near his jeans pocket.

There were so many feelings surging around my insides and none of them were good. My heart ached for Junior and I wanted Lisa and Trey to be okay. My soul lamented for the distance between Michael and me. I wanted to feel anything but those things. I wanted the suffocating feeling to go away. I still hadn't been able to breath normally since seeing the accident scene and then getting that awful news.

I shocked myself when I reached for the third button on his shirt and undid it. And then the fourth and on down. I opened his shirt and slid my hand over the short, knotty black chest hair around his nipples and then down toward his belly button. He just stood there.

Suddenly I pictured the Bev I saw in the mirror when I was waiting for him to return my credit card. The one with her hair down, the daring, risk-taking woman I had never met. She was back for a visit and for the next few minutes she took over.

I playfully pulled and twisted the hair near his belly button before sliding my finger into the hole just beneath his right pocket. He let out a shallow breath, but still just stood there. He was leaving it all up to me, so I continued. With my right hand still twirling in his pocket hole, I ran my left hand up his left leg until I found the button on his jeans; I undid his button and then his zipper, and then he took over.

He gently pulled me close enough so he could unfasten my jeans and slide my pants and underwear down to my knees. I kicked off my right sandal and slid my right leg out of the jeans. He lifted my leg, pressed me against the door, and within seconds started giving me what I needed. Slowly at first, then harder and deeper, until I cried out. I grabbed his shoulders to push myself up against the door frame and pull him deeper. I could feel the tears running down my cheeks as I let myself enjoy it. The pleasure overpowered the guilt and pain. I closed my eyes and got lost in it. I ran my hand over the top of his head, over the short plaited hair, but yanked my hand away. The hair gave identity to the feeling. I didn't want to attach a face to it. I just wanted the feeling.

When it was over, he didn't speak and neither did I. I pulled my clothes on as he fastened his pants. I tried to steady myself before I reached for the door handle, but there was no steadying. My knees were shaking, my head was spinning, and I felt like throwing up. I could taste the return of my last meal in the back of my throat. I pushed the door open and ran out. As soon as I got far enough away, I opened my mouth and let go of the choking remnants of something I had eaten early this morning or late that night. I wiped my mouth, but didn't look back. I wanted to run, to leave it all behind. I wanted to leave him, and the guilt. I wanted to leave it there, in room 209. The tiny room with a bathroom, a laptop on the table, and stonewashed jeans still lying over the chair.

Chapter 19

When I got back to the suite, Michael still wasn't there. I was glad. I undressed and got into the shower as if the steamy hot water could wash away the thoughts, the guilt. The water was hot, but not hot enough, so I turned the cold water off and let the steaming hot water torture my body. It hurt. I deserved it. I wanted to punish myself for all of it—for being so childish with my family, so negligent with my children, and now my infidelity. It was all too much as the water burned my skin and tore the scab off the flesh that had been torn the night we were robbed.

After the shower, I dressed and waited for Michael. It was four in the morning when sleep finally took over my body. Michael was still not in. I assumed he got a hotel room to avoid the awkwardness of dealing with me. As much as I wanted to do something to bridge the gap, I couldn't find the strength. I didn't have the strength to fight for my marriage in the midst of mourning the death of my son.

I made a pot of coffee as the sun slipped up over the horizon to give just enough light to the kitchen to allow me to see what I was doing. I didn't want to turn on the lights. The darkness was easier. The coffee dripped slowly, too slowly as the door flung open and

Michael walked in, threw his keys on the coffee table, and flopped down on the couch. He hadn't stayed at a hotel—he had likely slept in the car, or not slept at all.

I made him a cup of coffee: two tiny drops of cream, two teaspoons of sugar. I handed him the cup, but I couldn't join him on the couch. He sipped as I took a seat at the kitchen table, looking out onto the balcony, down toward the river.

No words were ever spoken. Grace called and we made plans to take care of last-minute funeral details. Michael's parents called from the airport. He left to go to meet them. Still no words between us.

While Michael was gone I called Grace to talk to Lisa. After batting back a few serves of monosyllabic grunts, we ended the feeble attempt at conversation. I tried to let Lisa know we were busy taking care of things, without talking about things we were taking care of. I wanted her to jump in with her hip teenager talk, but she barely gave the yes-and-no answers that let me know she was still on the other end. She finally made some excuse about Grace calling her and we both hung up with a simple, "Talk to ya later."

When Michael got back from the airport, he spoke to me for the first time since the awful time before the more awful incident with Victor. Part of my reason for calling Lisa was to get my mind off what had happened.

"We need to pick out the casket. You can ride with me."

Picking out caskets was enough to get my mind off anything, I thought. I nodded at him without making eye contact, grabbed my purse, and followed him out the door. During the drive to the funeral home, there were still no words. I wanted to speak. I opened my mouth several times with well-planned words, but none ever came out.

We pulled up at the funeral home. The same place where we had spent our Friday morning. The same funeral guy and money lady met us at the front door and that same lame-ass music was playing as we followed the funeral guy into the casket room. I could feel my throat tighten as if someone were choking me. We made our way into a room with caskets lined up around the wall. There were at least twenty rectangular boxes in various sizes and varying details. As I scanned the lines of gold, silver, and bronze colored boxes, they all gave off an impersonal aura. The boxes meant nothing without contents inside them. That was the connection—the precious cargo inside. A few of the caskets were open to reveal soft blues, pinks, shades of mauve, and pale green fabric with lacy details around the edges. The fabric looked soft, as if it mattered. I touched it to make sure it was soft, because it mattered to me. I walked around the room, touching delicately woven fabrics of soft blues not meant to show or draw attention. The mere presence of the boxes commanded attention. Everyone knew what they represented.

Michael still didn't speak, not even to the funeral guy. He walked and touched as if that was what we were supposed to do—survey the choices like a new car buyer strolling down the rows of the latest automobiles to hit the market. The funeral guy pointed out a few choices and talked about rust-resistant finishes and protection from the elements. None of it mattered, so I pointed to one. This wasn't searching for the perfect prom dress or a new outfit for the big dance. I needed to get out of that room, the room of boxes. There was nothing good about those boxes. Nothing.

We went back to the hospital to check on Trey. The nurse let us know that he was up and acting like he was feeling stronger. We knew both his legs were broken, but nothing prepared us for seeing him so bandaged and helpless. As bad as he looked, I fought back the tears, wishing Junior were lying in a hospital bed instead of the box we had just picked out for him. Grace walked in while we were visiting with Trey. She filled us in on his latest prognosis as only Grace could do. Part of me wondered how she could be in so many places at one time. Trey would be starting rehab as soon as he healed. He was in for an uphill battle, but he seemed happy to be alive, and remorseful when he mentioned Junior. Everyone had been tiptoeing around the subject. I didn't expect a seventeen-year-old kid to know what to say. So again, three adults and one teenager twitched nervously at the mention of the subject we would be forced to face in a matter of hours. When we left the room, Grace let us know the doctors were going to patch Trey up enough so that he could attend the funeral.

Michael's family met us at Grace's house when we were done at the hospital. Grace's place had become the main attraction, just the way she liked it. Lisa had found a way to get away from the house before Michael and I arrived. The idea of what was happening to us frightened me, but there was too much going on at the moment for me to concentrate on the future. I walked around Grace's place, surveying the decor as if I'd never seen it before. I dreaded the conversation with the Lamarks. I didn't want to tell the story again. I didn't want to hear their questions, but I knew that wasn't fair. There were grandparents, cousins, aunts, and uncles. They deserved to know, to hear, to mourn.

After as much rehearsing of the tragic events as I could stand, Grace and I went to meet with some other guy at the funeral home about transportation. I don't know why we couldn't handle everything at one time, but I didn't have the strength to fight it. Grace drove and I sat dazed, trying not to think about anything in particular while being bombarded with troubling thoughts of everything: the accident, my marriage, my infidelity, the land sale; I wanted to scream, and I did, but only inside, the quiet torment of a wounded soul too weak to beg for help.

The next funeral guy was too peppy for what he was required to do. We were talking about limousines and hearses, but he acted as if I were Cinderalla renting a limo for the ball.

"How many y'all got?" he threw at us while walking toward a fenced area full of long black and white cars.

"There's at least twelve in the immediate family, and then we want something for the kids and a few other family members," Grace blasted back at him, trying to keep up with his stride.

I didn't even bother to follow their pace. I just followed along, wishing to be anywhere but the back-side of this funeral home, looking at cars. The limousines all looked like throwaways from the white funeral home, but there was no way we could use anyone but Hampton and Sons Mortuary. We had used them for Mama and Daddy and everyone else in the Tayloe family who ever passed from life to death. And they never had decent vehicles. The one we finally settled on didn't look like it would start, much less take us safely from the church to the cemetery and back to Grace's house. After spending too much time looking at junk funeral cars, Grace and I made our way back to the inn to join Michael and the rest of the Lamarks for dinner.

The innkeepers had insisted on treating us to dinner at the inn restaurant. We were the only ones in the place that Saturday afternoon. On any other Saturday, Andre's would have been packed to capacity with guests standing all around the inn porches waiting to get in. But not this day. This day was for us. Chef Andre prepared the finest cuisine, starting with an appetizer of pasta shells stuffed with ricotta cheese, served with a fresh tomato basil sauce. Even though the mood was somber, the food was excellent and I managed to eat a few bites simply because it looked and smelled so good. There was a choice of two entrées: an herb-grilled chicken breast topped with imported capers in a champagne sauce or Norwegian salmon. After dinner, Andre served dessert and pleasant conversation as the mood lightened even more. I sipped a coffee and smiled as family members caught up with each other's lives. Lisa had managed to dodge us again. Grace said she was at the hospital with Trey. Despite the warm atmosphere and good food, the sickening feeling was coming back as I let the thought of the next day sink in.

My wristwatch showed 8:30 PM as we filed out of the restaurant and made our way to our destinations for the night. Within hours, at daybreak, I would start the most difficult day of my life, but first I had to get through this night.

This time Michael joined me in the suite. For the first time ever,

I wasn't sure how to handle the sleeping arrangements. How would I lie in the same bed with him after what I had done with Victor? Michael still wasn't talking to me. I wondered if he had seen something. Had he seen Victor and me in the garden holding hands? Grace had seen us—maybe Michael had too. Or maybe, God forbid, he saw me going into Victor's suite. Even though we should have been going to bed, I perked a pot of coffee, knowing full well sleep was the last thing we would do the night before burying our son.

"Where is Bessie? Did you board her at the usual place?" I managed as we sipped coffee.

"Yeah, she's at Helen's still. I never picked her up after you guys left. I called Helen yesterday to ask her to keep her a few more days. She sends her condolences."

Michael was still being responsible, handling things and taking care of business despite his grief. Making sure Bessie was taken care of. Didn't he realize I needed him too?

"Evelyn called the house and left about ten messages, so I called her back and let her know what happened. She said something about your fall stuff being in."

Evelyn Michelle is my personal shopper. She works in Providence, Rhode Island, at Nordstrom's. I hate shopping for all that uppity stuff I have to wear at Michael's law parties, but Evelyn makes the process so much easier. When I shop, I like to hit the mall and get the latest jeans and nice sweaters that fit my comfortable lifestyle. But Evelyn let me know the first time I met her that my shopping "would not do for a woman with a husband in Michael's position at the firm." She took me on as her personal project, and now each season she gets all my dresses, shoes, and accessories for the upcoming events. In mid July, Evelyn was already pulling together my fall wardrobe. I sipped coffee and smiled as I thought about the kind of lifestyle that was so different from the way I grew up in Mississippi. Grace would just die if she knew I had a personal shopper.

"So, you sold the land. What are you going to do with the money?" Michael spoke again.

"We set up a scholarship fund in honor of Junior. It just felt like the right thing to do."

"Don't Bobby and Mabel need that money? I would think you'd give it to them."

"Yeah, they need it, but they'll be okay. We all have each other."

"Sounds like you guys made some progress. I'm glad to hear it," he added, getting up to freshen his coffee. He filled the cup again— two drops of cream and the sugar—and then took a seat on the balcony. Our conversation was over.

I was alone again. That's the way it worked with Michael. We had talked about what we needed to talk about as responsible adults, so that was it—no emotional talk about our feelings or how we were going to go back up the road without one of the only two things we really had in common.

Michael stayed on the balcony as I finished my coffee and made myself content with the fact that there would be no discussion of feelings, emotions, fears, and doubts. I made my way to the bedroom, undressed, and slipped in between the cotton sheets. The caffeine was surging through my bloodstream and holding my eyelids open wide. To my surprise, Michael came into the room. I could hear him taking off his shirt and shoes. He slid into bed beside me, but not right beside me. It was a queen-size bed and neither of us was a large person, so there was a lot of space between us. We had been distant before, but this was different. I wanted to reach over and touch him, and force him to touch me, hold me. My hand felt like lead as a tear crept down my cheek and landed on the soft, fluffy pillow under my head. My back was turned to him and, without looking, I knew his back was turned toward me. On this hot July night in Mississippi, the room was dark and frighteningly cold.

I got up before Michael and pulled out the dress Grace had gotten for me to wear to the funeral: a plain black dress with long sleeves, despite the warm temperatures outside. Grace insisted on something to cover my arms. Churchwomen have this thing about covering stuff, so I didn't argue. I looked at the dress until I no longer saw the long, black, A-line polyester fabric, but instead a baby bassinet—the baby bassinet Mama gave me when she found out I was pregnant with Lisa.

I'd laughed when I saw that piece of junk, but it was the same bassinet Mama used with all of us, so she insisted on passing it along to the next generation. I took it despite my new-mom intuition telling me to get something newer and safer-looking. I used the oak wooden box covered with a layer of pink lacy crib bedding. I used it for Lisa and then changed the pink to blue for Junior. For whatever reason, after Junior was done with it, I couldn't get rid of it. After having two kids, I was eager to get rid of everything from maternity clothes to baby toys, but not that bassinet. I kept it, knowing I'd never need it again. It looked crazy sitting in the house with two adults and two toddlers, so when Junior was three years old, I turned it into a plant stand. I painted it a nice shade of light blue to match my decor and then let Lisa and Junior decorate it with their handprints and footprints. After so many years, I could hear the two of them giggling as they put hands and feet into paint and touched and stepped all over that bassinet-turned-plant-stand. I'd planted a number of things in that stand over the years, but today it holds a peace lily I picked up one day during those eight years when my family was heavy on my mind.

I kept my eyes closed as I stood up to slide the black dress over my head. The bassinet represented both a piece of Mama, each of my brothers and sisters, and my children. I pictured it sitting in the corner of my den in Melrose, close to the double-arm chaise, with the peace lily and its pointed leaves and occasional white buds that poked their heads out to give just the right splash of contrast to the sea of green. I took a deep breath, the first real deep breath I had taken in two days—a cleansing breath.

Chapter 20

I stood before the congregation of onlookers, friends, family, and coworkers from Massachusetts, and God only knows who else. I was shaking in my pumps as I looked out over the crowd. I've never cared much for public speaking and this was why. My mouth was dry and I was sure that if I opened it to talk, I would surely have that white milky stuff in the corners of my mouth in no time.

"I never really got to tell my son, Michael Jr., too much about Vicksburg and growing up in the South. He had visited Mississippi a few times, but there's a vast difference between visiting and living here." Someone shouted amen real loud.

"My two children, Lisa and Michael Jr., and I started out on our journey back home just five days ago. Three days ago, my youngest was taken from me as painfully as he was given to me. I labored for nearly twenty-three hours with Junior. Someone once told me there is nothing as painful as having a baby—well, today I know the one thing that's more painful: losing one." Listeners wiped tears and I glanced over at Michael, who wasn't even trying to hold his composure. He shouldn't have to, especially for his namesake. I glanced toward the back of the church and there was Trey in a getup that looked like a cross between a wheelchair and a hospital bed. His legs were bandaged just as they were at the hospital, but there were all kinds of cushions and pillows surrounding him. My guess was that they were there to absorb the shock of moving around in such a delicate state.

"During my long drive from Melrose, Massachusetts, to Vicksburg, Mississippi, I started to tell my kids about my family. I never really told them much about my family down here because we were so far away—my relationship with them had taken a bad turn, and I didn't think it would matter. But as I told them bits and pieces, I realized it does matter, because it helps them understand who they are."

"Preach, sistah," one man said.

Out of the corner of my eye, I could see a lady wearing a large red hat nodding frantically. The nodding and the red distracted me, but I managed to get my thoughts back to what I was trying to say—until I spotted Lisa pushing through the doorway. She had informed Grace that she wasn't planning to attend. We were all so busy with the last-minute things, no one took the time to look for her until it was time to load the family car. No Lisa.

"I didn't get to finish my little Tayloe family history lesson, so bear with me if you will as I tell my son, daughter, and nephew about a man who changed my life in ways I hadn't understood until this day."

"Junior," I said as I looked down at the casket. "Lisa and Trey," I said, looking toward the back of the church. A gasp rang out in the tiny, hot sanctuary. The spectators had been waiting to see the sister who was responsible for her own baby brother's death. I started back with my speech to help divert the attention away from Lisa, who looked more like a helpless cat on a ledge than a grieving big sister.

"His name was Johnston Tayloe, your grandfather."

I could see my brothers and Grace crying uncontrollably now as I started one of the easiest speeches I'd ever made.

"One of my father's greatest abilities was to make people see things in a different way. It didn't take long. He just told the truth, got to the point, didn't hold anything back, and got out of there. As I stand here in his stead, speaking the narrative of his life, I will follow that great example of truth, pointedness, and swiftness because I want you to see things differently. There are some things about him that I want you to understand as you have never understood them before."

I glanced at Michael. He still had a distant look on his face and tears in his eyes. I looked over at Andrew, and realized he too could benefit from this little history lesson about his father.

"There are absolutes. The truths that anyone with eyes and ears would have seen. He helped so many others and was generous his whole life. He gave away more than he kept. He toiled with the stretch of his back and the sweat of his brow from childhood to manhood. He put his family before himself. He was that rare breed of man who was honored to place his family first and offered spiritual and material provisions no matter what the cost." I paused as Grace shouted a good loud amen. Everyone who knew us also knew that Grace loved Daddy and he loved his little homemaker.

"See it this way, if you will: what it was like to be one of his girls. He had four women who called him—and only him—"the man in my life." Somehow, God infused in him the inexplicable ability to make each feel they had his full attention. I want you to understand that one man made four people feel as though they alone owned his universe. And he loved us. He loved us hard. He was delighted simply by our presence. He saw us through eyes glazed with adoration. He thought we were beautiful, when we were not. He thought we could create, when we were idle. He thought we were special, when we felt uniform. He thought we were limitless, when we felt designated. See it this way," I continued, as would-be mourners were now shouting amen loudly and frequently. I glanced back at Lisa who was no longer slouching in shame, but standing upright waiting for my next word.

"And honey, my father was fine. He was just as fine as summer wine. Listen to me if you don't know. The boy looked good." One woman shouted amen loud enough to draw a good deal of laughter from the congregation. "Well, y'all know he was good-looking—you know it," she said to explain her outburst. Several ladies in huge black hats agreed in a modest churchlike tone.

I continued. "And he was smooth with his. Let me tell you something: he was so fine and so smooth that he met this girl from North Carolina and made her switch states to be with him. And of course she was fine too—so fine, they stayed married for forty years and had five children who adored them. See it this way," I went on as all my siblings, even Mabel, chimed in with big amens and smiles.

"When you think of him, don't try to bring to the forefront either all of the good qualities or all of the bad. It's not right and it's not of God. You see, God created human beings. Innate in us, His own creation, are both the highest elevations and the deepest pitfalls, the ideal and the ailing. And if you saw this in my father, you are blessed. If you ever felt the tenderness of his love or came under the power of his wrath, you are blessed. If you ever saw him doubled over in laughter or shaking his head in disbelief, you are blessed. If you ever saw him change a person's mind swiftly with only the force of his words or relinquish a situation by throwing up his hands, you are blessed."

By now I was carrying that old singsong tune that Southern preachers use when they're about to bring it home in a good sermon. One of the preachers on the pulpit was making an annoying *mmmm* sound that almost threw me off. Family and friends were up on their feet shouting amen, and, "preach it, chile," as I finalized my family history lesson.

"If you bore witness to these things, the duality, you bore witness to his very humanity. And it is, I promise you, the perfect blend of poetry and prose. And when you think of him later, I think you need to say, 'Thank you, Jesus'."

After preaching about my daddy, I went on down the line with Mama and Grace, Bobby, Mabel, and Andrew: Grace's compassion for those in need, Mabel's unconditional love that transcended every boundary, Bobby's charm and ability to make you feel like the most beautiful and significant woman on earth, and Andrew's intelligence, wit and never-ending faith in the power of the human spirit. By the time I was finished, the crowd was on their feet showing love and appreciation for a family who was finding their way back to their roots.

Ladies in big floppy hats and black dresses and men in dark suits were clapping and "getting happy" as I took my seat. Grace, Mabel, Bobby, and Michael were crying tears of joy. Andrew looked like he had met a side of his family he always had hoped really existed. As I took my seat, I glanced at the casket, then at Trey, fiercely clapping his bandaged hands. I looked toward the door where Lisa had been standing. She was no longer there. There was no sign of her anywhere as I quickly scanned the back of the church. I looked back at the casket, spread out across the front of the altar, surrounded by as many flowers as they could crowd into this tiny church. The crowd was still on their feet, shouting, "Thank you, Jesus" and "Praise the Lord." My family seemed uplifted as they praised the Lord and hugged one another. But suddenly all I felt was empty.

The final part of the funeral was too much for me. Since the preacher didn't know Junior, there wasn't much he could add except the same old, "God plucked a flower from his garden" sermon. That was always a stupid analogy to me. Why the hell did God need my baby? The church people used the God/flower analogy as if to say that God taking a loved one made it more bearable, or to dare you to question God. Well, that one didn't fly with me, so instead of making some huge, religious moment out of it all, I made my peace with the facts. The children were trying to get away from a bad family situation that night. Escape. I knew about that line of thinking all to well. They got alcohol. Why wouldn't they? If you look at commercials, all the cool guys and girls are boozing it up. I drank all the time in front of my kids, so why wouldn't they have been drawn to it? That's the example I had shown them. When I got the letter from Mabel and couldn't bring myself to respond right away, I got drunk. They got back into the truck to drive home, not fully knowing the risk they were taking. And at speeds near fifty miles per hour, they ran head on into an unsuspecting eighteen-wheeler. That was what happened. No big powerful God tiptoeing through the flower patch, looking for an addition to his bouquet. It was simply a big, bad automobile accident.

As the mortician motioned for the family to rise and file out of the church, I suddenly sensed Michael's unsteadiness.

"Are you gonna be okay, baby?" I asked him quietly, trying not to draw any attention to his condition.

He didn't answer. He wasn't going to be all right. His baby was gone. How could I have asked such a ridiculous question? I just grabbed his hand and let him lean on me to steady himself. Somehow I was the pillar of strength. Focusing on reality was giving me the strength I needed.

I've never been one to lean on fictitious ideology. I like to keep it simple and stick to the facts. I can handle tough things better that way. So as we all filed out of the church and made our way into the two limousines that were designated for the family, I kept my mind on reality.

Reality took me back to the newspaper article I had read when the kids and I stopped at the hotel. The one about the grandfather who left his granddaughter in the car all day. I suddenly felt that grandfather's pain. He only offered to take the baby to day care to help her parents out. He wasn't used to taking care of a little one, and the fact that the child didn't cross his mind was conceivable. Was he negligent? Was I negligent when my baby met with death in the manner he did? At this point it didn't even matter. I, just like that grandfather, had to face the harsh reality that my son wasn't coming back and there was nothing I could do about it. They could arrest me, the driver of the eighteen-wheeler, and the bartender at the inn, but the fact remained that my baby was gone . . . forever.

I could see the black tent surrounded by mourners who must've taken a shortcut to get to the cemetery, because they were already standing there waiting for us to walk up and take those infamous seats next to the big open hole in the ground. I smiled at the mortician's effort to cover the hole, as if the stark reality of burial would be lost if we only saw the green grasslike fabric draped over my Junior's final resting place.

I took my seat beside Grace with Michael standing right behind me, leaning all his weight on my chair. I wanted to get up and let him have the seat. Why don't they put seats out for the men? They just automatically assume men don't have a struggle when they lose a loved one. I tilted my head back and looked up at Michael. He was still distant.

Bobby must've seen Michael leaning because within seconds he was standing next to Michael with his arm on his shoulder. The gesture looked like a caring brother-in-law offering support, and it was, but not emotional support. Bobby was holding Michael up physically. Bobby knew Michael was a proud man and wouldn't want to show weakness even at a time like this. So he held him up, and let Michael keep his dignity.

"Ashes to ashes and dust to dust," the preacher continued.

I didn't care to hear this short, stocky man say words over my boy, so I tuned him out and looked around the graveyard. I couldn't see faces clearly. I wasn't sure if the bright sunlight was hindering my focusing mechanism, or if I was dreaming. I saw people, but I couldn't make out who any of them were. So I looked on farther into the distance. There were cars zooming by the cemetery, going about their daily routine. It was Sunday and I wondered where they could be headed on a Sunday. But nowadays people do just about everything on Sunday. Church might be the morning activity, but the afternoon could be filled with everything from a trip to Wal-Mart, to a round of golf. Life was going on outside the cemetery. Those strangers didn't stop their routine because my world had come to a screeching halt. I wondered if I'd be able to get back out and go to Wal-Mart. I wondered if I'd be able to laugh and share a light moment with friends. Nothing seemed funny enough to make me laugh, and I wondered if it ever would again. Things that used to make me laugh—funny movies I watched with the kids, good books by my favorite authors—all of it seemed meaningless. Right then, I just wanted to jump into that hole under the grassy blanket.

"Amen," I heard everyone around me say. Michael was tapping me on the shoulder to let me know it was time to say good-bye. Grace, Bobby, and Mabel were standing over the coffin with roses and more tears than a human being should ever have to cry. I joined Michael and Andrew. I looked at the coldness of the box surrounded by all the bright reds, yellows, blues, and greens of the flowers sent by strangers and loved ones. The box represented death, yet all that was alive around it bowed to it, saluted it, and respected it. A nice lady in a white nurse's uniform handed us roses. I stood there waiting for someone to tell us what to do. There was no way they expected me to say good-bye.

If someone had told me two days ago that my son would be killed in a terrible car crash and I wouldn't even get to say good-bye, I wouldn't have believed it. No parent should have to deal with this kind of death. This little flower ritual they wanted me to participate in was not going to cut it. This was no good-bye, not for the comical kid who had spent day and night filling my heart with pleasure. Kids did that. They made a house a home. They brought life and vitality to a place. The phone rang every ten minutes and they were always arguing about something: "Who ate the last cookie and left the pack in the pantry?" or "who took my CD off my dresser?" It was always something. Always alive. What was left for me now? Why didn't I get to say good-bye?

As I fought the tears, I looked over to my left and caught a glimpse of my parents' tombstones. I hadn't realized that we were burying Junior so close to his grandparents. I tried to look away, but my head wouldn't turn. My feet wouldn't move, so I looked and read my father's tombstone. The last thing I wanted to do was think about the emptiness that my parents' death created in my heart. It was all so meaningless. Nothing in life seemed to matter at that point. What had it all been about?

BLESSED ARE THE PEACEMAKERS, FOR THEY SHALL BE CALLED THE CHILDREN OF GOD and OBEDIENCE IS BETTER THAN SACRIFICE—the two scriptures on my father's tombstone. For the first time in my life, I read those words and wanted to know what they meant.

Daddy was a peacemaker. He was criticized for it, but he was just living the Bible. He lived the life of a peacemaker in front of us as an example. Anyone can be confrontational and stir up a mess, but it takes a bigger person to foster peace. And obedience *is* better than sacrifice. Mabel said it perfectly concerning the rift between the Tayloe children: "Ya'll know Mama and Daddy ain' raise us to act like this." Obedience to the lessons we learned as children growing up had always been the answer to the problem. Working together in love, and keeping the peace. Obedience was hard sometimes, especially when it went against human nature, but sacrifice was often harder, because you didn't always get to pick the sacrifice. The Tayloe family had sacrificed too much for its lack of obedience. Junior was gone, as was the land Johnston Tayloe had worked so hard for. And the answer all along was simple communication: "If you have a misunderstanding, don't stop until you get an understanding."

"Thank you, Daddy," I whispered silently as I lay my rose down on Junior's coffin. Understanding that message for the first time didn't add to my guilt, it helped to erase it. And I made a commitment to stop running from the inadequacies in my life and face the truth head on—no more hiding, in my life or my writing. I rubbed my hand across the smooth surface of the box that would serve as a vehicle to the world beyond. The box that covers, shields, houses, honors, and stops time. I watched as the careful hands of the funeral workers lowered it into the six-foot-deep pit. I stayed until the box disappeared, the box that always commands a second glance, as a reminder of how fragile life really is.

The walk back to the limousine felt like it was a mile long.

Strangers and a few familiar faces were staring at us as if they were waiting for something to happen. Surely we wouldn't gather together, bury a teenage boy, and not show off. No one fainted, no one had to be carried out of the church wailing and lamenting. They certainly expected a show now that we were all forced to leave a child in this cold, damp place. But nothing. Bobby and Grace held on to Mabel, but she must have been sedated because she just walked whichever way they led. Andrew was walking and holding Chrissy's hand, and I . . . I was walking beside a man I once knew as my husband. Suddenly he felt more like a stranger, like one of the unfamiliar faces in the crowd.

Just as I got to the limo, I looked straight ahead and just a few feet in the distance stood Victor Mabrey. I couldn't respond to his presence, not outwardly. It wasn't appropriate. The brief eye contact lasted at most ten seconds, but it communicated volumes.

I took my place in the limo beside Michael. We didn't hold hands. We didn't even look at each other. I sat, trying not to think about the reality of driving off and leaving Junior behind. I remembered his first day of school, and driving off from that kindergarten and leaving my baby with someone else for the first time. That feeling hits a mother like no other. You know you have to let them go, to grow, to mature, but you know they'll be back. The limo sputtered and spat as the engine finally turned over and we slowly drove away, leaving him behind. This time he wouldn't be coming back.

We all gathered at Grace's house after the funeral, everyone except Lisa. There was more food and noisy people than should be allowed around a family in mourning. I smiled and did the small-talk thing as long as I could. All they could talk about was who cooked that good fried chicken.

I looked around at the sorry lot and my eyes fell on nasty-ass Bigun Spinks. He had the nerve to be sitting up in Grace's house like he was welcome. Just months earlier he had been bad-mouthing my entire family.

"Y'all—y'all got any more of dat cornbread? These chitterlings shole would be better wit some cornbread," Bigun begged.

"Look, fool, I can't even believe you had the gall to step up in here after what you said to Mabel."

"I . . . I . . . Beverly, girl, you ain' spose to talk to de elderly like dat," he retorted.

"Well, get your elderly ass out of my sister's house. And you aren't getting any cornbread with your chitterlings. What does this look like, some kind of restaurant or something?"

Bigun rolled his eyes and got his fat stinky behind out of the kitchen. All of Grace's church people who were serving the food seemed to appreciate my Northern charm. A couple of them winked at me as I left the room to chat with Grace.

Grace and I went to her bedroom to talk. She had something on her mind. I think I talked to my sister more those couple of days than I had my whole life.

"Bev, I'm gonna take Mabel in here with me. Those pills aren't really what she needs. She just needs us right now. Trey is going to need a lot of attention too after rehab. I'd feel better if I could look out for both of them. Besides, she's not getting any younger and projects-living ain't for old folk."

"You got that right. Maybe after you get her settled and eating and talking again, you two can come to Melrose for a visit—my treat."

I thought Grace's lip was going to fall off. She smiled and fought back the tears and couldn't say a word. We hugged and I made my way out of the lacy, frilly room that epitomized my big sister Grace. Mama picked the perfect name for her. All those years I hated her for being what we called her every day.

After leaving Grace in the bedroom, I said a few words to Andrew in passing. We agreed to talk in a week or so about the scholarship fund and get the ball rolling on that. He introduced me to his lady friend. She was beautiful. She looked just like one of those models in a magazine—the healthy models, not the anorexic ones. Andrew smiled from ear to ear as I gave him the thumbs-up.

"Go by the old Tayloe land before you head to the airport. There's something there for you," he whispered in my ear.

Bobby was standing outside on the porch as Michael drove off. I looked at the car heading out of the tiny neighborhood in east Vicksburg. He was headed back to the airport and back to Melrose. We were supposed to leave together as soon as we could round up Lisa, but for whatever reason, he was gone. I could only handle one thing at a time, so I just nodded and tried to maintain the funeral smile: lips slightly parted, turned up just a little at the corners. Folks can't tell if you're going to break out in laughter or tears. He was gone and I didn't feel anything. I had lost so much; I couldn't feel anything at that moment. Pastor Shorty had given us a pamphlet about grief after we met with him to make the funeral arrangements. One portion of the pamphlet talked about the divorce rate being higher for couples who've lost a child. The problem was not so much the issue of two people grieving, but two people not grieving together. I knew the distance was not what Michael and I needed, but I had neither the energy nor the heart to chase him. I'd deal with it later.

"Bobby Tayloe, why are you standing there looking just like Daddy?"

"Well, gotta make sho you get off safe and sound."

"We're gonna be just fine, don't you worry none."

"You know I'm gonna worry anyway, always have. You know I don't mind doin' what I have to for you, even go as far as breakin' da law." He laughed heartily as we hugged for the first time in too many years. And it felt good, real good.

Just as Bobby and I finished our tender moment, my cell phone rang. It was my editor. He apologized end over end for bothering me, but he wanted to offer his condolences. Michael had told him what had happened so they wouldn't fire their top mystery writer.

"I just want to say how sorry I am to hear of your loss, and you can just give me a call whenever you get back home and get settled, Mrs. Dunn," he said nervously.

"My name is Lamark, Beverly Lamark, and I'll do you one better—I'll meet you in your office in a week or so. I've got a story that will knock your socks off." I laughed.

"You've been writing? But I thought you'd be busy with . . . family things," he stumbled.

"I have and like I said I have a story for you. Life is one big story, and it's time I tell mine, and somebody's gonna listen this time." I smiled as I hit the END button.

It was time for me to make my way back to my life, but there wasn't much of a life to go back to. I wasn't sure what was going through Lisa's mind or if I'd have the strength to find out right away. No more Junior and his messy friends leaving junk all over my house despite my grandest efforts to keep things looking decent. I'd return to Michael working long hours, dinner parties with people who would become my best friends in my next novel, and too many lonely nights wondering *what if*. As I thought about it, I concluded that there was no hurry, really.

I got one of the sisters from Grace's church to take me back to the inn so I wouldn't have to bother my brothers and sisters with my troubles. They had enough to deal with in getting Mabel situated. I didn't bother to get the lady's name and it didn't seem to matter. She ran her mouth all the way to the inn, and I just smiled and shook my head, hoping my response fit her banter. Apparently so, because she kept driving and talking.

I thanked her, offered money for gas, and made my way to the garden out front where the innkeeper's wife stood.

"Would it be okay if I keep the suite for a few days? I'm not sure I'm ready to leave yet," I said.

"Sure, honey. If there is anything you need, don't hesitate to ask. I heard through the grapevine that you're a famous writer. Are you staying on to work or just relax?"

"I'm not sure. I'm just staying on."

As she walked off, Victor walked up from the back porch of the inn. He was still hanging around. Somehow I knew he would be. I wasn't sure I wanted to see him again. There were so many things I didn't feel like dealing with, and he was one of them.

"Leaving?"

"Not yet. This place is where I need to be for now. Doesn't feel like time to go yet. I'm surprised you're still here—I thought your work wrapped up days ago."

"Yeah, I'm not sure why I'm still here either. My next assignment doesn't start until Wednesday, so I decided to just stay here. Southern inns aren't usually my style, but, well, honestly, I really wanted to see you again. To say good-bye."

Those weren't exactly the words I wanted to hear, although I would never have admitted it. I wanted Victor to help me find the answers and fill the gap that had been there for so many years, but I had better sense than to think this was some kind of fairy tale. I had lost my son, was emotionally losing my daughter, and now my marriage. No, fairy tales don't end like that.

"But I'm here for a couple more days. Is there something I can do for you?" he asked.

"As a matter of fact there is. My family just sold some land down the river a piece. Can you drive me over there?"

We talked the entire time it took to get to the old Tayloe land. It sounded funny calling it the old Tayloe land. It seemed like it had always been our land, and when Daddy bought it, I'm sure he thought it always would be. Didn't quite work out that way.

"Sorry, Daddy," I whispered to myself as we turned down the dirt path that led to the land.

When I first got to Vicksburg nearly a week ago, that land was the last thing I wanted to see. Now, I was practically coming out of my seat as we rounded the curve.

"What exactly are we looking for?"

"I have no idea. My brother told me to come out here before I left town."

The land was all grown over with weeds and bushes everywhere. I rolled the window down because I knew the farther we drove, the closer we were to the river and by afternoon you could catch a good breeze off the Mississippi. Andrew had explained to me where they were going to extend the highway, but it had been so many years since I had driven down that dirt path, I couldn't really picture where they would put a road—until I saw the sign.

There it was in big bright red letters: FUTURE SITE OF THE JOHNSTON TAYLOE MEMORIAL HIGHWAY. Although Victor had no idea what that sign meant to me, he pulled over, stopped the car, got out, and walked around to open my door. I got out and stood there. It was just a sign. The road wasn't there. The new construction was months away, but it was my sign—a sign of the past and of things to come. I stood there reading the sign, which led to a new road for the folks of Vicksburg, and a new road for Beverly Lamark.

Victor and I didn't go straight back to the inn. Somehow, after seeing the sign on our old land, my spirits were lifted and I wanted to do something other than sulk about my misfortune. There were still a few things to be thankful for and I was committed to finding them. Although it was Sunday evening, the day's last showing of *Gold in the Hills* hadn't started yet, so we headed there. I sat through the melodrama and laughed, cried, and acted just like a woman who was losing her mind. I don't remember most of the drama. My mind drifted from my kids, to the fight with Grace, to Michael driving off without saying anything. My emotions were all over the place and through it all Victor was there. He didn't offer words, only a tissue during my crying fits. When the drama ended, we walked around the cemetery and I told him all about my father. He seemed genuinely interested, although I knew he was just trying to be sensitive to my fragile state. After the cemetery, we went to an ice cream parlor down the street from the inn. I ate some of my mint chocolate chip ice cream cone, but most of it ended up in the trash as I remembered summers in Melrose with Junior and Lisa.

After we got back to the inn, I apologized time after time for my erratic behavior. My crying in public and laughing without telling him the joke had to be embarrassing, but he still didn't seem to mind. I was just glad to laugh so soon.

He was only planning to walk me to my suite and leave me to my thoughts, but he stayed with me when I lost it at the door. It's amazing how it hits you sometimes. I opened the door to the suite and planned to turn and thank Victor for his company and say good night. Well, it didn't work out that way. As soon as I opened the door, I smelled it—the cologne Junior begged me to buy for him on our last trip to Saks Fifth Avenue. I could smell it strong, like he had just doused it on himself before going to the mall with his friends. He was starting to become such a little man. Victor tried to get my attention, but I had to find the source of the smell. I walked from room to room until I came across the little T-shirt. It was lying in the corner of the room Lisa and I were going to share. I hadn't seen it there before. Too much had been going on. I picked it up, sat down on the bed, put it to my nose and held on to my memories of him again. It was all I had and in that moment it was enough. Victor shut the door and left me to my insanity, sniffing a teenager's T-shirt, wanting more than anything to have one more minute, one more second.

I'm not sure how long I'd been sniffing the shirt when I realized Lisa was standing in the doorway. She had been so distant the last couple of days and I had been so distracted. I didn't know what her expression meant or whether I should try to find out. I resolved that the distance was bad and we needed to break through the walls now or our relationship might suffer irreparable damage.

"Have a seat, sweetheart."

"I won't be long. I took a cab from Aunt Grace's. Just wanted to see what's going on with you and Dad."

She felt like a stranger instead of my own sixteen-year-old daughter. I motioned again for her to join me on the bed. She again declined.

"They took my driver's license because of the drinking. Aren't you going to ask me about it?"

"I've been trying to give you time. So much has happened so quickly, baby."

She started pacing around the room but stayed near the door. I watched her stride, wondering what she wanted me to say about the drinking. I didn't have the strength to lash out at her. I was afraid to. I didn't want to chance something slipping out about Junior's death.

"I know you got some drinks and beer here at the inn. And your dad is handling things with the insurance company and the police about the accident. That's what he does, you know—the law," I said, hoping to lighten the mood.

No such luck. She stopped pacing, looked at the T-shirt, and started pacing again.

"Is he coming back?" she asked.

"I don't know and I can't think about that right now."

"But you have time to think about that other man, the one with the dreads. I saw you with him the day we got here. Are you cheating on Dad?"

Her words rang in my ears. To my knowledge Grace was the only one who knew about Victor, and her questions had been about how good he seemed with me, not about cheating. But that's exactly what it was. Nonetheless, it wasn't something I planned to discuss with my sixteen-year-old daughter.

"He's a friend. I met him the day we got here and he's been a perfect gentleman all along. End of discussion."

"So you're just gonna stay down here and walk around the garden with him and not even check on Dad?"

"Listen, Lisa—as if this is any of your business—your father is a grown man. He chose to leave, not me. And I resent your tone."

With that she jerked closer toward the door of the suite, but I reached her before she could leave. With Junior's shirt still in my hand, I begged her not to walk out in the middle of a discussion. She stopped short of the front door, put her hands on her hips and looked more like me than I had ever seen her in the past sixteen years.

"I learned it from you. Walk out when the heat gets turned up. Turn to the bottle when the pressure is too much. Now look what happened—I killed my own brother," she yelled, with tears streaming.

The door slammed behind her as the T-shirt fell from my trembling hands. All along I had felt responsible for what happened that Thursday night, but mainly because I wasn't exercising parental control. I had never focused on my own drinking and poor crisis management as possible causes. I looked down at the shirt on the floor. I fell to my knees, realizing that if something didn't change, I was about to lose another child.

I pretty much spent the night right there on the floor with Junior's shirt and my own sorrow. It was all too much for me to handle, so I pushed it aside and tried to do something, anything, to get my mind off the cold harsh truth that Lisa had thrown in my face the night before. Victor called and asked me to join him in the garden. I wanted the diversion. We sat in the garden sipping tea and then walked down by the river as the sun perched higher in the sky, raining her heated rays down on us. I told him about what Lisa had said the night before. He didn't offer his opinion, but just listened to me ramble. He took my hand into his. I thought about Grace's words the night before the funeral. I thought about the last seventeen years and before I knew it, Victor and I were walking along with our arms around each other. We strolled, the water rippled, and my heart fluttered—and I didn't try to stop it. When Lisa's words or harsh face crossed my mind, I shoved them out and focused on the good feeling. I had felt bad for long enough.

Victor and I ended up at the piano bar in the inn. I still didn't have an appetite and alcohol was the last thing on my mind, especially with Lisa's words still swimming around in my head. I couldn't even remember the last time I hadn't needed that crutch. The piano player hit the keys with soft, even strokes, Victor rubbed his thumb along the back of my hand, and the intoxication of the moment surged through my bloodstream. I didn't need alcohol, and I made up my mind: I would do whatever it took to get it out of my life, even seek professional help.

"You probably need some rest. Let's get you settled in for the night. I know you don't feel tired, but it's been a long day."

He was right. I could have sat there all night. But it had been a long day.

"Sleep might do me some good. I haven't been able to sleep since I got here four days ago."

We left the inn lobby and walked back toward my suite, hand in hand, just like it was supposed to be that way.

"Let's do breakfast in the morning, in the garden down by the river?"

"Sounds like a plan. I'll see you there," I whispered as he gently kissed my cheek and left me standing in the doorway.

I unashamedly watched him walk away. Yes, I was checking him out. I didn't care who saw it. I realized that true enough, he was attractive, but it wasn't anything physical that was drawing me to him. It was his soul beckoning to me. I thought of Grace's words again and smiled. I went inside and slept.

The next morning Victor was waiting in the garden with breakfast just like he promised. We ate and talked. And, at moments, we sat in silence, letting the river speak. We held hands and strolled through the gardens we had missed the day before. My senses seemed keener. I saw things in nature I'd never seen before. Just walking along, I could smell the sweetness of the flowering buds; I could hear the buzzing bumblebee landing nearby to take a sweet dip. For the first time ever, I could feel all the things I had been trying not to feel.

I called Grace to check on Lisa. Grace let me know everything was fine and gave me an update on Trey. She had moved the rest of Mabel's things and officially made her a resident. I let her know that I wasn't alone, and that I would contact Michael later. She didn't press me for any information and I didn't give any.

I went back to the cemetery. Victor went with me. I wasn't sure I wanted him along at first. As far as that part of my life was concerned, he felt like an intruder.

"Bev, if you don't mind, I'd like to know what he was like. I didn't get a chance to meet him and, well, if you don't mind. . . ."

It felt awkward, but the more I talked, the more I realized that that was exactly what I needed to do. I wanted to tell someone about my baby. I wanted someone to care about the simple, silly things. I wanted to tell someone how much I felt like we had failed my parents. I had spent eight years away from my brothers and sisters and there was no way to get that time back. I felt guilty. I needed to say it. And he listened.

The day lingered on and again I was in and out of emotional peaks and valleys. I wondered if every day would be like that. Victor and I had dinner at one of the casino boats on the river. We strolled along the downtown streets, looking into the shops and laughing at the tourists who visibly didn't fit in with the Vicksburg crowd. After another day, another series of seconds, minutes, and hours, we went back to my suite. This time Victor joined me and we shared that iced tea he had mentioned the first day I met him.

I felt closer to him. This time when we made love, it was not the dirty, guilty lust that overtook me at his door the night before the funeral. This time it was the result of spending so much time together and sharing all the things I wanted so desperately to share with Michael. I even found myself thinking about Michael while I was with Victor. That was strange, but I didn't try to figure it out. I had spent seventeen years with Michael, and there was no question that he was still a part of my life, my thoughts, and my heart.

Victor stayed with me the next couple of nights as I went from crying crazy woman to passionate lovemaking machine. Several times I started to call Michael. I even dialed the number and let it ring twice, but hung up before he could pick up the phone. I needed to know how he was doing, but I didn't want him to know how irrationally I was behaving—sleeping with another man just as if I weren't a married woman. Each time the guilt of my infidelity bombarded my thoughts, I played the grief card. I'd just lost my son, so everyone should turn their head and ignore the adultery. Besides, they had no idea of the weight and pressure I was dealing with whenever I sat still enough to think about what had happened and how my life had gotten so screwed up.

Chapter 21

After two days of taking in the sights and sounds and sipping sweet iced tea with Victor, I was ready to write again. My senses were alive and I couldn't wait to get a blank sheet of paper in front of me. I walked down the street from the inn to the convenience store and bought ten blank notebooks. I almost jogged back to the inn, eager to start pouring thoughts onto those blank pages.

My writing career had come full circle. I was hundreds of miles from the laptop computer, printer, and modern technology that adorned the "cave" in Melrose, but I had my notebooks. There I was, sitting in Vicksburg, Mississippi, with a pile of notebooks and a wealth of imagination. I started writing and I didn't stop to notice that the sun had gone down and there was barely enough light in the room to see the paper in front of my face. My eyes had adjusted to the lack of light and I was still writing. Had it not been for the knock on my door, I probably would have written until the paper disappeared into the darkness.

"Hi, did I disturb you?" Victor asked.

"Oh, not really. I've started on my next book—come on in."

"I don't want to bother you. I can just come back later—well, not later, because I'm leaving in the morning."

I had forgotten Victor was scheduled to leave for his next assignment. I didn't want to be rude on his last night in town, but I really wanted to get back to my writing.

"Listen, don't let me stop you. I'll just be on my way. You look like you're really going at it," he said, looking at all the notebooks and sheets of paper scattered around the suite sitting area.

"No, Victor, come in, it's really okay. If you don't mind me doing what I do, I don't mind the company."

Victor came in and made himself comfortable. I turned on some light and went right back to the notebooks. I was writing like a mad woman and filled another ten pages before I realized he was staring at me.

"I don't mean to stare, but it's just incredible to see this. I've read all your books and it's just awesome to see you doing what you do, with such passion."

The word passion swam around in my head as he went into the kitchen to get a drink. The passion was back and I felt like I could write all night and still not say everything I needed to say. The words just wouldn't stop coming. I thought back to the empty paper in Melrose before I started off on this life-changing trip. I looked around at the notebooks and paper and realized I wouldn't have enough paper to get it all out. The feeling was overwhelming.

"Can I get you something?"

"Yes, I'm actually ready for a break. Well, not really, but I would like for you to read some of it."

I shocked myself with that statement. I had never let anyone read my freshly written work, not even an editor. My first draft was always so raw and unorganized, just random thoughts spewed out on paper. But I needed to share it with him. I needed to let someone read my soul.

"Sure, I'd love to read it. Where does it start?" he asked, looking around at the jumbled mess that was all over the floor and couch and kitchen table. "Never mind, I'll find it. You just keep writing."

He only had to say that once. With a quick sip of iced tea, I was back at it again. I was writing so fast and furiously that I was sure he wouldn't be able to make out most of the words. This fury of activity went on for at least another two hours and then I realized I should probably eat something.

"Are you hungry?" I asked.

"Yeah, I'll run over and get something from the main house. You keep working."

I couldn't have asked for a better response. That was exactly what I wanted. When he got back with the food, I wished he could feed it to me intravenously so I could keep writing, but I stopped the flow long enough to swallow a few bites. I was chewing and swallowing but my mind was still on the papers in front of me, when he walked over with a napkin and gently patted the sides of my mouth. Normally the gesture wouldn't have fazed me in the least, especially when I was writing, but this time was different. He was less than six inches from my face, looking into my bloodshot, weary eyes. I couldn't help myself. I leaned over and kissed him—not passionately, but enough to get his attention.

"Okay, you're just going to keep on surprising me, aren't you?" he said.

I smiled and leaned closer and this time I didn't hold back the passion. I wanted him with the same intensity of desire that I wanted those pages filled with words. This time was different. I wasn't responding to an attractive man or the caring friend who had spent the last few days by my side. This time it wasn't about Victor, or sex. He stood up, as if trying to adjust to what was going on, but within seconds he was down on the couch as papers flew in all directions. I was certainly the aggressor, but he soon caught up with me.

"Bev, I don't want you to think I'm trying to take advantage of your—"

"You couldn't take advantage of me. I need this."

Loose pages of thoughts, feelings, and emotions crumpled under the weight of our lovemaking as we moved from the couch to the floor to the kitchen. I could see flashbacks of all the horrible things—

the robbery, the accident, the funeral, selling Daddy's land—and I had to let all the pain out. He helped me get it out. I had carried the weight of the world around on my shoulders and years of not measuring up in my heart. I was tired of hiding. I wanted out. I wanted to be free. He helped me find freedom. I didn't allow my mind to operate at all. I just went with the feeling—no rational thinking to make me stop, to make me feel bad for needing this.

Chapter 22

"Hi, Grace, this is Bev. What ya doing?"

"Not much, are you still at the inn?"

"Yeah, I'm at the inn. I was just wondering if I could come to your place for a few days, just until I figure out what next?"

"Girl, you know you don't even have to ask. Come on."

"Okay, I'm on my way."

She didn't ask any questions although I know she had a million. That was Grace: crisis management. And I was in crisis. When I got to her house, she and Mabel were having coffee and talking about a bunch of nothing. Lisa was at the hospital with Trey.

"Mabel, girl, Halle Berry is black," Grace insisted.

"Yeah, Grace, but she ain' black like us. She too pretty to be jes black like us," Mabel insisted.

We all laughed, knowing what she meant. Halle Berry is Mabel's favorite actress. Mabel was asking Grace about renting Halle's latest movie for her. But of course Grace didn't have a VCR, so that's where I came in. A trip to Wal-Mart is inevitable when three sisters are together for more than a couple of hours. We picked up the VCR, nearly twenty dollars' worth of fattening snacks, and made our way to the video store.

Mabel insisted on the Halle Berry movie, so Grace and I decided we'd each choose something by our favorite actresses too. Grace loves Michelle Pfeiffer, but really needed a Clint Eastwood fix, so we got *The Bridges of Madison County* for her. I have to see something with Angela Bassett when I'm down in the dumps—talk about a strong black woman. I grabbed *What's Love Got to Do with It*, not even concerned about what the movie would suggest to my sisters. Grace just smiled and Mabel started looking for something—anything—with Denzel. With movies in hand and hope in our hearts, we hurried home for a chick-flick night. We tore open bags of chips and cheese puffs and put ice into big cups, as Grace's annoying grandfather clock started singing its tune of seven ominous chimes.

"I say we watch *Monster's Ball* first, before Mabel has a fit," I suggested, licking salty potato chip crumbs off my fingers.

"I second that," Mabel chanted.

"So, let it roll," Grace ordered as I pushed the tape into the machine, turned down the lights, and grabbed a twenty-ounce bottle of Coke.

Certain parts of the movie got to me, but it was okay because I was surrounded by the safety and security of my sisters. I cried with Halle when her son died, and I cried some more when she reached out to Billy Bob to help get rid of the pain. When the movie was over, we all agreed to go ahead and get a box of Kleenex and keep it near the snack bag.

After a bathroom break, it was time for Angela Bassett. More drama and tears. This time it was Mabel who was on the emotional roller coaster. I wasn't sure what her problem was, but being a mom without her babies, I knew it didn't take much to start the river flowing. When the movie ended, Mabel didn't move. She didn't get up to get more junk food or tissue or take a potty break. She just sat there.

"Y'all, can I tell you somepin?"

"Yeah," both Grace and I chimed in unison.

"I ain' never tol nobody, but Trey daddy beat me too, jus like dat man on dat movie. He beat me bad, y'all, real bad," she sobbed.

It took her another few seconds to get herself together, so we just waited.

"I was seven months pregnant, and he beat me so bad, I almos los Trey. One of da girls in da projecs called da ambulance and dey took me to da hospital, but I tol em not to tell y'all. I los a lot of blood and everything, but Trey was okay. He made it, beatin' and all."

Both Grace and I grabbed her and almost smothered her, trying to make up for the pain of carrying that around all those years. She had blamed herself for almost losing Trey. She didn't want anyone to know she was beaten because she really loved Trey's dad. She was ashamed of it, but she did. So that night, sixteen years after the beating, she let herself come to terms with all of it. And she freely cried about the accident. No drugs or tranquilizers this time—with Grace and me by her side, she mourned a whole lot of things.

Bobby's knock on the front door almost scared the living daylights out of us. We had been so caught up in our own stuff, we didn't realize a car had pulled up in the yard.

"Look like y'all havin' a party or . . ." He paused, realizing we were all crying.

We couldn't help but laugh. There we sat, with junk food wrappers and soggy Kleenex all over Grace's fancy den furniture.

"I ain' mean to botha y'all, I jes wanted to check on da Tayloe gals, and look like y'all doin' jes fine," he said laughing on the way back out the door.

He had pushed the door open and was almost out, when he stopped as if he had just thought of something.

"Ya know, dis is all I wanted, jes to see y'all like dis again," he said, his voice cracking as he let the door shut behind him.

We watched him as he got into his car and drove off. After a quick break, it was time to lighten things up with a little Denzel. We all needed that.

After the Denzel movie was over, Mabel announced she was going to bed. Grace put a kettle on the stove and pulled out a couple of tea bags. We sat there in silence until the kettle started whistling.

While Grace was in the kitchen making tea, Lisa walked through the door. She looked at me and then around at the fancy room covered with chip bags and soda bottles. I looked at my watch and it was 1:30 AM. I didn't comment about the time and the fact that she couldn't have been with Trey that late. Grace walked in with two cups of steaming hot chamomile tea. She sat one cup down in front of me, and the other on the end of the coffee table in front of an uncomfortable-looking chair. She nodded her head for Lisa to sit. She didn't look back at me, just said good night and left the room.

I knew where this was heading and I could only put it off for so long. Lisa sat down just as if Grace's nod was the prompting she needed. She sipped her tea and looked straight ahead.

"How is Trey?" I asked.

"Pretty good. They let me spend the night sometimes, but I decided not to tonight. He likes having me there. I guess I need to be with him. It helps when I start missing Junior."

She continued sipping and looking ahead. I watched her body language. Besides being tired, she seemed at peace. She still hadn't made eye contact with me.

"I feel bad about having to sell the land," I began. "We should have done something to keep it in the family. We are all intelligent enough to have made something out of that land, something that could have kept our family alive. That's what your grandparents would've wanted."

Lisa finally looked at me, but didn't speak. She sipped and looked straight ahead, and then back at me.

"I haven't heard from your father. I'm sure you have. I started to call him, but I wasn't sure what to say, so I didn't. I've been with Victor—the man with the dreads."

She shifted in her seat and forced her eyes onto the wild patterns on Grace's walls.

"The night before the funeral, I tried to reach out to your father and he, well—it didn't work so I went to Victor's suite. I regretted it at first, but after Michael just left, less than an hour after burying Junior . . . well, I'm not sure it was such a bad thing."

I couldn't believe the words that were coming out of my mouth. I was being too honest with my teenage daughter. For the first time ever, I was talking to her just like another adult woman. And I knew it was the right thing.

"Where is he now? You gonna leave Daddy for him? I know you and Daddy aren't happy together. Doesn't take a brain surgeon to figure that one out."

"I have no idea. I spent the last couple of days and nights with Victor at the inn. But he left this morning and I have no idea how to get in touch with him. Well, I could, but I won't. He didn't leave a number or a note or anything. He just left while I was asleep. I have his business card from when I first met him, but I won't call him. He's not that type."

"Who was he? Where did he come from?"

"He's a photojournalist for *Newsweek*. He travels, mostly to other countries, but occasionally he gets assignments in the States. He was doing a piece on the old Vicksburg Bridge. He's never been married and says he never will be. I don't know where he lives and it doesn't matter. He was what he was. I can accept that. It hurts that he didn't want more, but I got what I needed from him, if that makes sense."

"I guess it makes sense. So what about Dad and us? Our family?"

"I don't know about that either. Like you said, things haven't been good between us for a long time, and, well, I just don't know if there's anything there for me. My life in Melrose was you and Junior. Your father and I drifted apart a long time ago. I'm just not sure we even have a marriage. If he wants out, I'll let him go."

"I saw you with that guy the first day. You were smiling and acting silly. You've never acted like that with Daddy. Why?"

"I'm not sure why." I was almost taken aback by her question and

I wanted to shut down, but I knew she wanted the truth, so I continued to be honest with her.

"I always felt silly for wanting your dad to want me, so I just tried to be content with what was there. I assumed he never wanted it—the passion, the romance, me acting silly, as you say."

"What do you want, Mom?"

"That's the part I'll have to figure out."

"Yeah, I guess we all gotta do that," Lisa added, finishing her tea.

She got up, walked toward my seat, and kneeled down. She laid her head in my lap and I ran my hand through her hair.

"Yeah, we gotta figure it out," I whispered as the grandfather clock in Grace's living room spilled out two loud chimes.

Chapter 23

During the next few days at Grace's, I played back some of the things that had happened in the last week. The letter from Mabel, the ride from Massachusetts to Mississippi, the robbery, and that song that was playing when we first got into the truck Tuesday morning a week and a half ago: "Lord don't move my mountain, just give me the strength to climb." I remembered hearing that same song in church as a kid growing up and how stirred-up the crowd got when the song started. Several ladies in the front row would "get happy" and lose all their dignity. As I thought back on that song during my adult years, I always said it didn't make sense. If I had a mountain in my way, I'd rather have it moved—who wants to climb some damn mountain? But that was my ignorance talking.

The weeks after the funeral were filled with mountain-climbing days and nights. Between my crying fits and eerie silence, I mentioned crazy things like moving to Maine, cutting all my hair off, and swimming every day. That wasn't going to happen. I hadn't learned to swim.

Lisa and I visited Junior's grave site often. I didn't feel awkward. I finally understood what visiting the dead was about. It had nothing to do with the corpses in the ground, but the living corpselike people still walking around trying to make sense of their lives. My visits were less frequent as the days went by.

The Lord didn't move my mountain. I was climbing every step of it. I missed my son. I still loved Michael. I wanted my daddy's land back. Many days I wanted to just let go and fall into the abyss of nothingness, but I held on. I closed my eyes and remembered my climbing from the day before and I put one foot in front of the other and pulled myself up. There was no other way to know how to climb a mountain than to climb it. I knew the slippery spots that set me back. I knew the crevice that I could anchor myself on and gain ground. So, each day I climbed, I learned, I grew.

Lisa and I stayed at Grace's house for another couple of days, not knowing what I would do when living with my two sisters got to be too much for me. I had picked up the phone at least ten times to call Michael, but made some kind of excuse each time. Lisa was talking to him at least every other day. I had no idea where to start, and the more time passed, the more I felt like I would never figure it out. While Grace and Mabel were doing their thing, I spent my days writing. I'd visit the grave site or Trey at the hospital, or go to the gardens at Cedar Grove and write. The weather was nice and I must have been getting adjusted to the heat, because I spent hours outside in one spot or another, writing, editing, and rewriting.

My publishing company was willing to work with me when I informed them that Beverly Bradford Dunn had officially retired. I introduced them to the new kid on the block; Beverly Lamark, African-American fiction writer dealing primarily with family saga, love stories, and an occasional romance. They weren't crazy about the change, but at least I had paid my dues in the business, so they were willing to give it a try. They made an official announcement and everything, acting as if Beverly Bradford Dunn were a real person. They wrote up a big retirement announcement and sent out press releases to all the important people.

I was putting my things into my bag at Grace's, trying to figure out what to do next, when my cell phone rang. I automatically assumed it was my editor calling to get the ball rolling on my premier novel as Beverly Lamark.

"Hey, Bev, baby—it's Michael. I need to talk to you."

"Michael, I'm surprised. I thought you were Jake."

"Yeah, I heard about your retirement. Are you still going to write or are you doing something else now?"

"I'm still writing. What else would I do? It's all I know. Nothing else makes sense, right?"

"Yeah, I suppose so. Actually, Bev, I'm in Vicksburg and I need to see you. Can you meet me at that inn where you were staying?"

"No—oh, I don't mean no, just not that inn. I can meet you someplace else. What about one of the restaurants downtown?"

"Yeah, well, I have Bessie with me and as well mannered as she is, I don't think they'll let her into the restaurant."

"Okay, but not at the inn. Just meet me in the garden district, down the street from the inn. I'll be there in ten minutes."

I could feel an excitement and apprehension. I wanted to see him. I needed to see him, but I wasn't sure what would come of the conversation. Why did he bring Bessie? Was this the end, officially?

I was there in less than ten minutes, and he was standing by one of the many wading pools in the garden district. Bessie was curled up around his feet. He almost didn't look like the same man. He had lost weight and he was dressed as casually as I'd ever seen him. He was actually wearing a blue pair of Dockers and a Fubu T-shirt. *Where did he get Fubu?*

As I got closer, I realized it was one of Junior's shirts. I had to stop because the sight was making my knees go weak. He watched me. We stared at each other. A quick flash of Victor's face crossed my mind's eye. I tried to ignore it, but it was there. I wanted to hide it from Michael, but that's not the way it works—not with husband and wife. Nothing could be hidden; no matter how hard you tried, it was still there, the good, bad and the ugly. He reached for my hand. I continued walking toward him. I wanted to feel some-thing—something to give me a sign of what I should do. I wanted to feel the sensations I felt when I first met Michael in that park in Cambridge. I wanted his quirky smile and strong cheekbones to grip me the way they had that first time. But all I saw was sorrow, grief, pain, and a tear rolling down a not-so-strong cheekbone.

"Bev, I'm sorry I just left like that. I was hurting and I didn't know what to do. I saw you. I saw you with him the night before. I saw you coming out of his room."

"Michael—"

"No, Bev. Let me finish. I've got to get this out. I know I wasn't there for you all those years. I've been in Melrose this past week trying to figure it all out. I never wanted to hurt you. I worked hard all those years because I love you and I thought the harder I worked, the more I could show you that love, you know, with things. I never wanted you to want or need anything. I grew up poor and I re-member too many nights lying cold in a bed, wondering if we'd get to eat the next day. I know you were struggling too when we first met, so I was determined we'd never have to go through that again. And I got lost somewhere in there."

I had never seen him like this. In seventeen years Michael had never let his emotions show—not this kind of emotion.

"Bev, when I walked back into the empty house in Melrose, for the first time I understood what you were begging for from me all those years. I was working hard to make sure you never wanted for anything, and all along, you wanted me. I know I pushed you away. After losing Junior and then seeing you with him, I knew I had messed up. I left because I didn't know what else to do. A man needs to be able to fix things and make them better. I couldn't fix it. I couldn't bring my boy back, and I wasn't sure you wanted me any-more, so I walked away."

"Michael, so much has happened and most of it isn't good . . ."

"I know. You don't have to tell me. I can see it in your eyes."

"I just don't know if I can do it. I need time—at least time to figure out what I need to do."

"All I'm asking is that you give me a chance to win you back. Help me figure it out. Help me figure out how to love you the way you need to be loved, baby girl."

He hadn't called me "baby girl" in years. During our months apart after we met in Cambridge, Michael would call me and end each conversation with, "I love you, baby girl." Even if he forgot to say it, I'd remind him because I loved hearing the way he rolled off the *rl* in "girl."

He picked up Bessie, handed her to me, and the three of us hugged. We went to the cemetery together and put a fresh bouquet of flowers on Junior's grave. We dropped Bessie off at Grace's and had lunch at one of the restaurants downtown.

We sat in the restaurant with food in front of us, but neither of us ate. The conversation was awkward at first, but then after he caught me up on everything he had done in the last week, I realized he wanted to talk more about us—our relationship.

"Do you need anything, any money or anything? What am I talking about—you make plenty of money."

"I don't need money, but this conversation . . . this is good."

"What are you gonna do now? Where are you going?"

"I'm finishing up a book. I'm going to New York in a few days to meet with Jake."

"No more faceless author stuff. Why?"

"Just tired of hiding."

He nodded at my confession, still shuffling food from one side of his plate to the other.

"You should eat something. You're wasting away," I said with concern.

"Can't eat. Doesn't feel right yet."

He fought back the tears, but I didn't. I shouldn't have had to. We sat in silence until the waitress concluded we were not there to eat and took our plates.

"Listen, sir, ma'am. This one's on me. You didn't eat anything anyway. You're the writer, right?" the waitress asked.

I nodded, trying to dry my tears with the linen napkin.

"I heard about the accident. I'm sorry. You all have a nice day." She smiled as she walked off to take water to another table.

"What about Lisa? The drinking?" Michael asked.

"Monkey see, monkey do. I haven't had anything to drink since the funeral, and I don't think I will. But if the taste comes back, I'll get help. Lisa's a smart girl. She just needs the right example. All teenagers do."

He nodded at my confession. I knew he wouldn't bother Lisa about the drinking. He'd handle the legal issues, help her do whatever she had to do in order to get her driver's license back, but that's as far as he'd go with it. The rest was up to me.

"I saw the sign, over at the old family place. That's pretty neat. Naming a road after your dad."

"Yeah, not too bad, I guess."

"Listen, I haven't moved anything in the house. Everything is still just the way it was when you guys left. I figured we could do it together—you know, go through everything."

"Yeah, we can do that."

As we walked out of the restaurant back to the car, I wanted to grab his hand, to touch him and let him know there were still feelings. I reached my hand out, but it felt like it was too soon, so I adjusted my purse on my shoulder and got into the car. During the drive back to Grace's, Michael kept talking, giving me fragments of what he had been doing. I hated myself for not being able to tell him what I had been doing.

"I called a few people, like the school, Dr. Holbrook, and the SAT people called about an incomplete form. I guess Lisa forgot to fill out something when she took the test. I handled it and she can settle the rest when you all get back."

"Of course you did."

"And you have a problem with that?" he questioned.

"No, I'm just saying that's how you are. You handle things. You take responsibility for stuff. You provide for people. And I just need more." With me on the brink of tears again, we pulled up to Grace's house.

He stopped the car, turned off the ignition, and tapped his hand against the steering wheel.

"And I wanted to give you more. I just don't know how sometimes, baby girl."

He had said it again. My mind went back to my conversation with Lisa. Michael didn't know how to give me what I needed, but he wanted to. The question was whether or not I had the courage to try again. That was something I needed to figure out.

Grace and Lisa were standing in Grace's front doorway. Lisa walked to the car holding Bessie. I was glad to see both of them since Michael and I had slipped into one of those awkward silent moments again. As Lisa made her way to the car, I sat battling with my emotions. Part of me wanted to just touch his hand, and part of me wanted to get away from him, too ashamed of my actions since the funeral.

Michael took Bessie from Lisa and gave her a hug. They said some things to each other while he put the cat into the carrier. I watched him as Lisa said her good-byes and blew kisses at Bessie. I felt a slight flutter in my heart. As Michael placed Bessie in the car, I noticed that he barely filled out Junior's Fubu shirt. Lisa jogged back toward the house to give us a few seconds of privacy. She had decided to stay with Grace while I wandered around the city writing like a mad woman.

Our problems weren't worked out and we weren't leaving Vicksburg together, but my heart felt lighter, better than it had in a long time. I reached into my purse to get my keys. And there it was, at the bottom of my purse along with rocks, dirt and gravel. It was the compact Michael gave me on our tenth wedding anniversary. I thought it had been stolen the night of the robbery. But there it was, still covered with some of the dirt from that night. I rubbed my hand over the inscription as Michael got into the car to leave. 10TH ANNIVERSARY . . . BEVERLY AND MICHAEL . . . FOREVER.

"What's that?" he asked, still moving stuff around to get settled for his long drive.

"Oh, nothing really, just my MacGuffin." I smiled, flirting from my heart.

He smiled. After seventeen years with a mystery writer, he knew I had found a missing clue.

"I'll call you," I whispered, seeing that quirky smile on his face. That smile that had changed my life, in a park in Cambridge, so long ago.

"Take your time."

I tossed the compact back into my purse and turned to walk to my rental car. I glanced back and caught Michael sneaking a peak at my booty. So I gave him a little extra hip action as I got into the car and took a quick look in the rearview mirror. A smile stretched across my face as I mouthed an almost silent "baby girrrl."

MISSISSIPPI BLUES

CASSANDRA DARDEN BELL

ABOUT THIS GUIDE

The following questions are intended to enhance your group's
reading of *Mississippi Blues* by Cassandra Darden Bell.
We hope the book provided an enjoyable read for
all your members.

DISCUSSION QUESTIONS

1. Beverly is unfulfilled in her marriage, yet something obviously attracted her to Michael. What were those things that drew them together, and are they enough to keep them together?

2. What role is Beverly's estrangement from her siblings playing on her state of mind at the beginning of the book? What impact is that breakdown having on her relationship with Michael, her children, and her career?

3. Despite her career success, Beverly is still an unhappy person. What about her own character and personality is feeding her unhappiness?

4. Grace, Mabel, Bobby, and Andrew all play roles in bringing Beverly to revelations that change her outlook on things, from the initial heated confrontation to the somber end. What are each of their roles? Who was most instrumental in helping Beverly find herself?

5. What role did Beverly's upbringing play in her transformation? Discuss her memories of growing up—her father, mother, siblings, and neighbors in Vicksburg. Have you ever had to revisit the past in order to find your way in the present?

6. What are the things that drove Beverly into the arms of Victor? After being regretful of her infidelity, what caused her to go back to him again after the funeral?

7. There have been cases in the courts where parents are held responsible for their underage children's drinking if a crime is committed while the child is under the influence. Discuss Beverly's parental responsibility in the case of Lisa drinking, driving, and causing a fatal accident.

8. Why did Michael leave without discussion after the funeral?

9. Studies show that the death of a child can cause enough emotional strain on a relationship that spouses often sepa-

rate and eventually divorce. What do you think will ultimately happen to Beverly and Michael?

10. Discuss Beverly's symbolic "coming out," both as a writer and a person. Have you ever come to the realization that you were hiding in some area of your life? How difficult and important was it to reveal your true self?

Please turn the page for a preview of
AFTER THE STORM by Cassandra Darden Bell,
coming from Sepia Books in 2005

After the Storm

by

Cassandra Darden Bell

Paying off a debt could easily be described as "better than sex." And the larger the debt, the better the sensation. My mind was all over the place as I stepped up to the end of one of three lines forming at the front counter of Southeast Bank. On most days the sight of the three old men and the woman pushing the baby stroller in front of me would have put a sour note on my day. That combination can turn a five-minute bank transaction into thirty minutes of pure hell—the old men shamelessly flirting and gawking at the tellers' cleavage as they cash their social security checks, and then the woman with the baby has to stop at least three times in the middle of her transaction to quiet the little tot. But this day, neither of those annoyances was going to ruin my mood.

"Is someone helping you?" I spun around only to see the top of her strawberry-blond hair. A short round woman wearing a navy blue business suit, whose double-breasted jacket buttons were stretching the buttonholes of her jacket out of proportion, gazed at me with professional concern. I caught myself giving her the once-over before answering.

"Yes, I need to see someone about paying off a loan and making a . . . well, a rather large deposit," I whispered, only wishing I could jump onto one of the deposit slip islands in the middle of the bank and yell it for all to hear, "For the first time in my life, I have a large deposit and I'm paying off my loan, early!"

But that would have been inappropriate, so I just followed the oval-shaped woman to an office marked CUSTOMER SERVICE. I noticed her tight calf muscles rippling with each step in her high-heeled blue pumps. She motioned for me to go inside and informed me that someone would be right with me. She smiled pleasantly and wobbled off to pounce on the next unsuspecting person to walk through the revolving doors at the front of the bank.

I had been in the customer service office too many times when I first started my business, either begging or almost begging for loans or extensions to already existing loans. But not this time. This time, I was in the driver's seat.

As I carefully planted my nervous behind into the leather seat, I noticed the office looked abandoned—no generic ocean prints on the wall, no framed pictures of the kids or the family pet, not even a pen or coffee mug to clearly say someone had been here and would be back. Before I could get up to find out if I had been put in the holding cell until the powers that be decided to attend to me, he walked in—dressed in an impressive black single-breasted suit with a white shirt and snazzy print tie. That clean-shaven-and-smelling-good, 6'2" hunk of a man made me forget my manners. His head was shaved as clean as a baby's behind and had a nice shine to it. His deep chocolate complexion looked like the part he didn't get through inheritance, but instead most definitely from long hours in the sun. It made me think of a Snickers bar, the new kind with almonds instead of peanuts. I caught myself licking my lips as he maneuvered around the office.

"I'm sorry you had to wait. I'm Ty Basnight. Ty, short for Tyrese—just moved to town from Raleigh, North Carolina . . . at your service," he said as he dropped a pile of papers on the desk and extended his hand toward mine.

I stood up and, not sure what else to do, shook his hand. He had rugged hands for a man in a suit who was working in an office. They had clean, even-length nails, but small calluses at the base of his fingers. Perhaps from gardening or weight lifting, I thought, as I started to tell him about my banking needs. But Ty Basnight was too far into his all-about-me speech, so I sat and listened as he fumbled with the computer and the pile of papers strewn in front of him. His accent sounded like a cross between Andy Griffith and intelligent, articulate blacks in the presence of equally intelligent white folk—big words with just a hint of Southern drawl. I wasn't sure of what he said because my mind was on the little red button on the side of the desktop computer—the tiny red button that would give the surge of power Ty obviously was searching for with no luck. After running his hand around the entire perimeter of the machine, he finally came across the button, flipped it, and kept running his mouth.

"Yeah . . . moved to town just a week ago. Still trying to figure out which one of those bridges leads to my apartment."

I giggled, acknowledging the bridge problem. I'd been in Jacksonville, Florida, all my life, and if my mind wasn't on it, I'd still take the wrong bridge. But I couldn't tell Mr. Basnight that because he was still yapping and fooling with the computer.

I assumed his nervousness was the cause of his rambling, so I sank comfortably in my seat and watched him fumble with papers, waiting for the electric dinosaur that had seen better days to power up and show some sign of intelligent megahertz. Since Mr. Basnight was in his own world, I gave the computer a good once-over and realized it was a Pentium 166 and, to make matters worse, they were using Windows NT. By now, Ty Basnight was deeper into his life story, waiting for something to pop up on his screen. Finally, a log-in screen came up and I almost laughed. Being a computer geek myself, I knew something Ty obviously did not. For whatever reason, the bank was running NT on a Novell network and no one had bothered to give Ty the password. I smiled as he discovered the problem and quickly tried to cover by shuffling those same damn papers he was tossing around when he came in.

He was handsome, with polished white teeth that shown bright against his dark skin—a mouth full of teeth that I might have time to count if he continued his rambling. He finally made eye contact with me after a few of the papers slid off the front of the desk and landed at my feet. We both burst out laughing at the first impression from hell.

I pulled my papers from the burgundy portfolio and slid them across the desk.

"I think this is what you're looking for."

"I must look like an idiot. They told me to come in and help you and handed me these papers that I assumed had something to do with why you're here. . . . But anyway, I'm sorry."

"No problem. This was quite entertaining. You shuffle papers and bullshit very well for so early in the morning." I giggled, knowing full well I was flirting with Mr. Basnight and his absolutely bare left ring finger.

I assumed, being a country boy, Ty would not catch my worldly sophisticated technique, but he caught it just fine.

"Well, you'll have to let me make it up to you," he added with an equally flirtatious tone.

Ty Basnight took the papers, read them over, and left the room to get the ball rolling on my payoff. He was in and out of the office, asking questions about the type of loan and payoff penalties. And the occasional compliment was raising Ty's score on the date-potential card. I got up from the seat in his "makeshift office" and looked out the door, hoping to see him coming with the final papers for me to sign. Instead, he was scurrying around with one of the tellers, looking into files and printing things from the main computer. He threw up his index finger indicating he would be with me in just a minute. As he and the slim teller in a flower-print dress walked off, I knew I had many minutes to wait, and for the first time in a long time, I didn't mind.